THE GENIAL DINOSAUR

Borgo Press Books by JOHN RUSSELL FEARN

*1,000-Year Voyage: A Science Fiction Novel * Anjani the Mighty: A Lost Race Novel* (Anjani #2) * *Black Maria, M.A.: A Classic Crime Novel* (Black Maria #1) * *The Crimson Rambler: A Crime Novel * Don't Touch Me: A Crime Novel * Dynasty of the Small: Classic Science Fiction Stories * The Empty Coffins: A Mystery of Horror * The Fourth Door: A Mystery Novel * From Afar: A Science Fiction Mystery * Fugitive of Time: A Classic Science Fiction Novel * The G-Bomb: A Science Fiction Novel * The Genial Dinosaur* (Herbert the Dinosaur #2) * *The Gold of Akada: A Jungle Adventure Novel* (Anjani #1) * *Here and Now: A Science Fiction Novel * Into the Unknown: A Science Fiction Tale * Last Conflict: Classic Science Fiction Stories * Legacy from Sirius: A Classic Science Fiction Novel * The Man from Hell: Classic Science Fiction Stories * The Man Who Was Not: A Crime Novel * Manton's World: A Classic Science Fiction Novel * Moon Magic: A Novel of Romance* (as Elizabeth Rutland) * *The Murdered Schoolgirl: A Classic Crime Novel* (Black Maria #2) * *One Remained Seated: A Classic Crime Novel* (Black Maria #3) * *One Way Out: A Crime Novel* (with Philip Harbottle) * *Pattern of Murder: A Classic Crime Novel * Reflected Glory: A Dr. Castle Classic Crime Novel * Robbery Without Violence: Two Science Fiction Crime Stories * Rule of the Brains: Classic Science Fiction Stories * Shattering Glass: A Crime Novel * The Silvered Cage: A Scientific Murder Mystery * Slaves of Ijax: A Science Fiction Novel * Something from Mercury: Classic Science Fiction Stories * The Space Warp: A Science Fiction Novel * A Thing of the Past* (Herbert the Dinosaur #1) * *Thy Arm Alone: A Classic Crime Novel* (Black Maria #4) * *The Time Trap: A Science Fiction Novel * Vision Sinister: A Scientific Detective Thriller * Voice of the Conqueror: A Classic Science Fiction Novel * What Happened to Hammond? A Scientific Mystery * Within That Room!: A Classic Crime Novel*

THE GOLDEN AMAZON SAGA

1. *World Beneath Ice* * 2. *Lord of Atlantis* * 3. *Triangle of Power* * 4. *The Amethyst City* * 5. *Daughter of the Amazon* * 6. *Quorne Returns* * 7. *The Central Intelligence* * 8. *The Cosmic Crusaders* * 9. *Parasite Planet* * 10. *World Out of Step* * 11. *The Shadow People* * 12. *Kingpin Planet* * 13. *World in Reverse* * 14. *Dwellers in Darkness* * 15. *World in Duplicate* * 16. *Lords of Creation* * 17. *Duel with Colossus* * 18. *Standstill Planet* * 19. *Ghost World* * 20. *Earth Divided* * 21. *Chameleon Planet* (with Philip Harbottle)

THE GENIAL DINOSAUR

HERBERT THE DINOSAUR, BOOK TWO

JOHN RUSSELL FEARN

Edited by Philip Harbottle

THE BORGO PRESS

MMXII

THE GENIAL DINOSAUR

FIRST BORGO PRESS EDITION

Published by Wildside Press LLC

www.wildsidebooks.com

DEDICATION

For Eleanor Rose King

CONTENTS

CHAPTER ONE
RETURN OF A MONSTER

Clifford Brooks, the rangy mining engineer with a thirst for adventure, had definitely made history when, in blowing up the base of a basalt area, he had accidentally loosed upon the world the monsters of the Jurassic Age. But now that was over. It had happened two years ago, and the last monster had been eliminated. Indeed, even more than this, the dangerous nitrogene gas escaping from inside the earth and threatening the destruction of humanity and perpetuation of the monsters had been sealed off. Yes, everything was very peaceful.

Well, almost. There was, of course, the usual daily talk of governmental and international upheavals; of the creation of new and deadlier weapons with which to destroy your next-door neighbour—and above all, there was the constant threat of alien invasion. The latter menace, though, was probably more the imagination of news writers who ought to have known better than a business to be taken seriously.

Proof of this invasion? Only strange flashes seen at intervals on the surface of Mars, and there was their possible tie-up with unusual objects glimpsed at times in the Earthly skies. These objects had nothing to do with flying saucers, and anyway they were differently shaped. Nothing like a saucer: wedge-shaped and moving at something like 18,000 miles an hour. The flying saucers of many years past had ceased to interest the public. Eminent high-ups had definitely proved them to be natural phenomena or the repercussions of indigestion, and that had to suffice. So, of course, this new business of wedge-shaped spots before the eyes moving at 18,000 m.p.h. provided something new for bored Mr. and Mrs. Everyman to talk about.

Not that Cliff Brooks was bored—hell, no. From being a first-rate mining engineer, he had graduated to that of chief consultant on mining and geology to the government's South Regional Division. It carried a thumping salary, a stupendous amount of work, and absolute promise of a nervous breakdown. Actually, Cliff Brooks had only himself to blame. With his wife Joan, and, several other engineers—who had lost their lives in the process—he had descended a thousand miles into the Earth. Therefore, he alone possessed the valuable knowledge that geologists were constantly requiring in collusion with the mining companies. And in these days, when man was having to dive ever deeper for his raw resources in the nature of oil, coal, and mineral ores, the knowledge was worth a king's ransom.

"Just the same," Joan said one evening, when Cliff came home looking as though he had been through an atomic washing machine, "you ought to take things a bit easier, Cliff. What's going to happen if you crack up?"

"I shan't," Cliff grinned. "I'm only young yet—far as vitality goes—and anyhow, I'd sooner risk cracking up and be worth a fortune than penniless and disgustingly healthy."

Joan was silent. There was something in what he said, of course. His money in the past two years had enabled them to own a delightful detached home outside London, had provided them with every necessity life could offer.

"Yet sometimes," Joan said, reflecting, "I rather sigh for the days we used to know. The little villa, you coming in full of bursting energy, me with the electric stove.... Remember the day you brought home the egg?"

Cliff did not answer for the moment. The mention of the dinosaur's egg he had once brought home from the underground Jurassic Region, which egg had later produced the fantastic, terrifying diplodocus known as "Herbert," was something he did not care to remember. Not because it filled him with horror: quite the opposite. He always felt miserable when he remembered Herbert. Poor, lumbering, eighty-ton Herbert, buried somewhere nearly a thousand miles down in the earth. Neither Cliff nor Joan could ever forget that they owed their very lives to the monster's colossal strength. Without him they would never have returned to the surface of the Earth and the blessed light of day.

"Stop making me miserable, can't you?" Cliff growled, as he headed for the lounge door to freshen up before the evening meal. "The past's finished with, Joan—and Herbert with it. At least I hope so!"

"You don't hope anything of the sort!"

Cliff paused at the door, looked back, then returned across the lounge to where Joan was standing. She was an ash blonde with hazel eyes—a most feminine girl, with plenty of courage, but not over-quick on the uptake, which was probably why she was so appealing.

"You dare to question my statement Mrs. Brooks?" Cliff asked severely, gripping her shoulders.

"I do, sir! You know as well as I do that if Herbert were to come romping across the ground of this wilderness of a house of ours, you'd be the happiest man alive! I know I'd be the happiest woman, anyway."

"This is absurd," Cliff muttered. "What kind of chumps are we, Joan? What in blazes have we in common with an eighty-ton beast from the prehistoric age? It's ridiculous!"

"Not a bit—just natural love of animals. Doesn't matter how big he is. We're fond of him, and he's fond of us. Not easy to forget an old friend when you've reared him from an egg."

"The egg that you thought of using for omelettes!" Cliff reminded her; then with a gentle tilt at her chin he added: "And now I've really got to get changed, sweetheart. Can't be as Bohemian as we used to be now there are servants around."

Joan nodded and smiled absently, gazing outside on

to the peace of the summer evening; then presently she glanced at the clock, saw it was time for the tele-news, and pressed the button on the remote control. An immaculate announcer with an impeccable voice merged into view on the large flat screen.

"...can be discounted as nothing more than meteor strikes on Mars and atmospheric aberrations on Earth. Dr. Handersley thereby disposed of the prevalent myth that danger might threaten us from the planet Mars. If that were really so, the danger would indeed be extreme since, as yet, we of Earth have not completely—"

Joan yawned a little and settled herself on the chesterfield. Same old story. Threat of invasion from Mars being explained away by yet another of the so-called experts in the scientific field.

"From the region of the Scottish Highlands," the announcer resumed, "there are reports of slight earth tremors. These are being experienced over an area of perhaps fifty miles, and seismologists and geologists are of the opinion that their cause is land subsidence some thirty miles down.... In the Commons today it was decided that a higher tax rate should—"

Joan switched off and yawned again. The heat of the summer evening was trying, and everything was so monotonous. For her, anyway. Cliff had his job to do, and therefore he was kept on his toes—too much so in fact. But for her things were slow indeed. Only this big house to supervise, a jaunt in the city now and again perhaps, and that was all. So different to the days when she and Cliff had been fighting for their lives a thousand miles down in the Earth....

Then after a while Cliff returned, spruced up, but still looking like a man who is doing too much. He glanced at his wristwatch as he crossed the lounge.

"I'm too late for the news, I suppose?"

"'fraid so," Joan responded, rising. "I got some of it, but there's nothing interesting—unless you'd call it interesting to hear that Dr. Handersley has decided that the so-called spaceships darting from Mars are actually atmospheric aberrations."

Cliff reflected. "Atmospheric aberrations, my foot!"

"What? You don't mean you actually *believe* the bunk about attack from Mars being possible? Why, everybody knows it's a dead world with nothing but deserts! We've been sending TV cameras there for goodness knows how long...."

"I only wish it *were* bunk, Joan, but I don't think it is. There may not be any actual *Martians* around, but what if beings from *another* world have recently landed on Mars? I've made a special point of studying the various reports on the matter—cold, dispassionate, scientific accounts without the unimaginative bleatings of the boys of the Press—and I think there may be something in it.... Nothing we can do about it, of course, but I wouldn't be surprised at anything which might happen."

Joan looked vaguely troubled, but said nothing. Cliff gave her a glance.

"Nothing else in the news worth having?"

"No—except for earth tremors in Scotland caused

by land subsidence thirty miles down—or something."

Cliff frowned. "That's queer. In fact it's almost unheard of. The Scottish Highlands are rooted absolutely deep, and the possibility of land subsidence, and thirty miles down at that, is almost impossible. Wouldn't surprise me if I'm not contacted about it for an opinion—"

He paused as there was a gentle tap on the door. Parkinson, the, manservant, was there to announce that dinner was served.

* * * * * * *

And away in the Highlands another dinner was being served—or it might equally have passed for supper or tea. It was, to be precise, the edible handout provided by the canteen of a mining contingent. Here, in the deeps of the Highlands, some forty miners and their engineering counterparts were based, probing for new sources of mineral deposit which instruments had definitely proclaimed were present.

So whilst Cliff and Joan sat in lordly and none too happy state in their palatial home, the mining engineers joked with one another in the warm summer gloaming, and ate the meal on the enamel plates before them. Cliff had often eaten his meals like this in the earlier days, and been a much happier man in consequence.

"Any ideas on that earth tremor business, Nick?" one of the men asked, and his southern accent sounded odd in these regions north of the border.

"None at all." Nick was the foreman of the outfit, and like everybody else in the unit, had heard the news over the field radio. "I certainly *felt* it, and it struck me that it wasn't very far from here."

"Do you suppose that our jabbings have had something to do with it?"

"Not a chance!" the foreman scoffed. "Why, we've hardly scratched the subsoil as yet, and this tremor was traced to thirty miles down and more."

"Come to think of it," one of the men said, pausing with a hunk of bread half way to his mouth, "I believe I can feel a sort of tremor at this very moment! How about you fellows?'"

The assembly looked about them in the gloaming. Away to the north and east the mountains had foundered into the purple of the summer night. To the south and west was rocky landscape, but it was more or less level. Here and there it was despoiled by mighty electric pylons carrying power, and the new McDermott River Valley Project.

Tremors? Yes, there was something, and every man could sense it, probably because every man was seated and thereby directly conscious of ground vibration. It was a curious, intermittent shaking which seemed to be coming nearer. Just as though a vast pile driver or trip hammer was being released at intervals, and being brought closer each time.

"What in blazes *is* it?" the foreman demanded at last, staring about him—but all he saw were the lights of the little 'portable' mining huts and domiciles and the brooding mountains grouped beyond.

Then for a space the concussions ceased. The men resumed eating, and talking amongst themselves, Nick included. Then, as he talked to the man nearest him, he suddenly froze in mid-sentence and stared in paralysed terror into the gathering night.

"What's the matter?" asked the engineer beside him, chewing methodically.

Nick swallowed and stared obliquely skywards. His mouth said; "Look!" but no sound came forth. His colleague gathered the drift and stared upwards. Then he too saw it and forgot everything else.

Infinitely far overhead, as it seemed, was a lizard's face. Or *was* it a lizard? It could have been some kind of sea serpent of stupendous proportions. No, it wasn't that, either. It was an animal of some sort with a head as large as a comfortable-sized dwelling house. The head was moving around slowly against the twilight sky, perched on the end of a thick, bulging neck. It appeared that there were eyes catching the faint after-glow from the west, eyes as big as soup plates.

"My God!" Nick whispered, and all of a sudden he shot to his feet and yelled at the top of his voice: "Take cover, boys! Animal of some sort watching us! Get the explosives over here quickly! Step on it!"

For a moment the rest of the men, except his immediate colleagues, wondered if he had gone crazy, a thought which was instantly dispelled as from the monster's cavernous mouth, with its triple rows of saw-like teeth, there shattered forth a ground-shaking bellow. Whether the noise was meant to be one of fury or just playful excitement, the startled miners did not know: what they *did* know was that the monstrosity was large beyond imagination, and that it was commencing to lumber down into their midst.

The men flew for their lives, not sure where they were going, not caring indeed just as long as they put a good distance between themselves and the monster.... And the monster ploughed onwards. It descended the short slope on which the miners had been resting, rocks crumbling to powder under the weight of the gargantuan clawed feet. Then, when it reached the clearing where the equipment—abandoned now for the night— was lying, the creature halted and sniffed the warm breeze. The noise created by this performance sounded like an old-time express train moving at full speed with safety valve open.

Cowering behind every available rock, boulder, and domicile, the engineers and miners had their first real vision of the monster that had come amongst them. They sweated, and gazed, and sweated again. The creature stood a good fifty feet high from ponderous feet to colossal head. His length was possibly a hundred and fifty feet to the tip of his broad, tapering tail, this in itself as thick at the base as any railway train. The back legs were short; the front ones longer and massive as grey pillars....

"I thought we'd bumped off all these damned things!" one of the engineers panted, glancing at his nearest neighbour. "It's one of those blasted prehistoric monsters that used to roam about a couple of years back— Remember the fun there was? Wonder where in Hades this fellow came from? He's the biggest I ever did see!"

The dinosaur obviously did not hear the engineer, so it must have been chance that moved him in his direction. The ground quaked, the engineers and miners fled again, and then the monster was walking casually through the midst of the domiciles.

They flattened like matchboxes, and where men were inside them, it was just too bad. Those who had been sent to get the explosives came courageously forward, dodging the vast feet and struggling to arrange detonators. The moment the huge beast had passed through the crumpled remains of the domiciles the explosives went off. Earth and debris blasted into the night to the accompaniment of blinding flashes and ear-shattering noises. But when all the confusion had died away, there was a vision, in the newly switched-on searchlights, of the dinosaur still going, head swaying back and forth as though he were trying to catch some particularly elusive scent.

"Warn the authorities!" Nick shouted, as the men began to converge upon him. "If that brute gets loose in a city, anything can happen. It'll be the former horror all over again!"

A man fled for the field telephone just as the dinosaur—now a quarter of a mile distant—walked through the midst of the overland wires and snapped them like cotton threads. So, back at the mining base, radio had to he used. Across the country the warning was flashed that for the second time in the past few years prehistoric monsters were prowling around. Well, *one* was, and that seemed to imply there might be others.

This, though, was an exaggeration. There was only the one dinosaur abroad. Otherwise, everything was peaceful, and the skies were free of flying lizards and pterodactyls. No, there was only this lonesome giant, ambling now across the rugged Highland countryside towards nowhere in particular, and at the same time coming dangerously close to the high voltage lines powering half of Scotland's cities as well as the McDermott River Valley Project.

The dinosaur suddenly became entangled with the cables. Down they came, the pylons snapping at their concrete bases. Glasgow, Edinburgh, and Aberdeen became partially blacked out, and desperate signals went forth to the maintenance engineers. From the McDermott Project engineers there also arose a cry for help. Millions of gallons of river water were relying on electric power to keep them dammed. If the power remained off for any length of time, the whole valley and generating station in the heart of it would be flooded out.

The giant from the Jurassic Age knew nothing of these things. He was only aware of shooting pains through his armour-like hide as the live wires whipped and flashed around him. He roared with fury and pain and then broke into a run, snapping the wires in the process. With this the pains ceased, so the dinosaur slowed up and moved with its former Juggernaut speed over the rugged landscape.

The hue and cry was terrific once warning had been received. Out came the militia and the air force. The peace of the night sky was rent in twain by the scream of jet planes. Pilots, mistaking shadows below for the monster, dropped bombs on private property and agricultural land, to the fury of the owners.... Red-faced commanders ordered guns to be fired at everything from a tree to a rock.... Nerves, naturally. The memory of the earlier invasion was still fresh in the minds of most people, and it produced something close to hysteria even amongst the ice-brained masters of army manoeuvre.

Daylight came early. Summer mists dispersed and warm sun poured forth. Courage rose. Planes by the hundred scoured and photographed the British Isles from end to end, but no signs of a monster or monsters were reported. The only assumption was that the mining engineers up in Scotland had tippled too much whisky and seen a pink elephant in a new guise.

And the blackout of Scottish cities? The broken pylons and telephone wires? The smashed miners' dwellings and the score or so crushed bodies? Scotch whisky could not account for this.... All very mysterious and perplexing. Better go on searching, then. In fact, a good time was had by all, and especially by the mighty brute about whom all the bother had arisen. It could not be located for the simple reason that it had blundered into an old mine shaft and there fallen asleep, partly underground.

But when night came it was on its way again. Farms were denuded of cattle and livestock to satisfy the brute's vast appetite. Entire ponds dried up to slake his thirst. And he went on remorselessly, yet with animal cunning enough to know that daylight might spell his doom. At the first sign of dawn he disappeared to the lowest level of land and there slept, secure in the knowledge that the fools of human beings would never distinguish his brown-grey colour against the similar hue of the countryside....

So, gradually, as day succeeded day, the exciting news of a wandering monster died down. It was believed to be all talk, probably to take the public mind off the ever-present though indefinite possibility of invasion from Mars. Just the same, certain people in certain places—namely, Westmorland, York, Derby, Leicester, and Oxford—did swear they had seen by night a mighty bulk against the starry sky. Southward, ever southward: this seemed to be the dinosaur's course.

The two people in all Britain most interested in the reports of the dinosaur were Cliff Brooks and Joan. They gathered all the news they could, but most of it was fragmentary. So Cliff made a special trip to Scotland and there talked with the miners who had first sent forth the warning. The fact they had also seen colossal footprints in the softer parts of the region—and the broken pylons and flooded McDermott Project—convinced him that *something* had indeed made its appearance from below.

"Did you by any chance get a clear view of this monster?" Cliff asked Nick anxiously, when general questioning and investigation had finished.

"Yes, Mr. Brooks." Nick gave a grim nod. "High as a three-storey building and heavy enough to make the ground shake. It's had me wondering since if maybe the earth tremors around this region were not caused by that brute pulling down underground rockery. I just don't understand it. I thought you and your wife, and those engineers who unfortunately lost their lives, sealed everything up to stop any more invasions from below."

"We did." Cliff gave a serious smile. "We took care to block up all monsters and pterodactyls—save one. That one monster was a diplodocus, the most fearsome of all prehistoric monsters. A brute weighing eighty tons. That one we *didn't* seal off—at least not intentionally."

"Oh?" Nick looked puzzled.

"My wife and I had a sort of affection for that one," Nick explained uncomfortably. "We reared him from an egg and he kind of took to us. We called him Herbert—just for fun. He pulled our borer free of disaster when all human agency had failed. Saved our lives, in fact. But on the way home—about eight hundred miles below surface—rockery fell between him and us, and we believed that was the end of him."

"Believed?"

"That's what I said. Now I'm wondering. Plainly,

this brute you have seen is a diplodocus, and far as I know the only diplodocus likely to be able to escape must be Herbert! It's all very harassing."

"Yes," the foreman engineer agreed, staring. "Very. First I've heard of this—making friends with a dinosaur, I mean."

"Why not? People make friends of tigers and elephants, so why not dinosaurs? All in the upbringing—"

To this Nick had no answer. He had heard from various sources that Cliff Brooks was overworking, and now he felt sure he had visible evidence of the fact. To talk in tones of the deepest sentiment concerning one of the most terrifying beasts ever known to exist just didn't make sense. Cliff, for his part, gathered from the foreman's expression what was being thought, so he did not delay any longer. He had learned all he needed, so the wisest course seemed to be to head homewards. Before he did so, however, he rang up Joan and gave her the news.

"Ten to one it's Herbert, Joan," he finished urgently. "If that is so, I don't know whether to be glad or sorry. If he's Herbert, he's liable to get us into a whale of a lot of danger; and if he isn't, there'll be danger anyway."

"We can discuss it when you get home," Joan said, and her voice sounded rather formal—so much so indeed that Cliff raised his eyebrows.

"Anything wrong back home, sweetheart? What did I do to merit the cold shoulder?"

"Don't be so silly, Cliff! It *is* difficult to say much,

though. The vicar's only in the next room!"

"Oh, him again!" Cliff made a wry face as he realised that genial, high-living gentleman had probably called for another fat subscription. "Okay—I understand. See you later."

Cliff rang off and back home Joan put the receiver down and returned into the lounge. It was just after five o'clock, and the torrid summer sunlight was pouring in upon the rotund figure of the Reverend Grimsby Maxwell, vicar of the parish to which Cliff and Joan belonged. His visits were disturbingly frequent, and by no means concentrated upon dispensing the gospel, either. The reverend gentleman had his heart set on a new church, and the wealthy Clifford Brooks looked likely for becoming the financial pillar thereof. All very well in its way, but Joan did have the feeling that the reverend was somewhat exceeding the limit.

"Not bad news, I trust?" The vicar beamed and balanced a cup of tea dextrously on a plump knee.

"Pardon?" Joan looked at him vaguely and then started. "Oh, the phone, you mean? No, it wasn't bad news—just my husband telling me about a relative of ours. Herbert, by name."

"Ah, I understand. I had rather hoped I would see your husband, as there is a little matter I would like to discuss with him." The vicar raised the tea and sipped it. "It concerns the new church annexe. He— your husband, of course—is so brilliant an engineer it occurred to me he might be able to help me."

"My husband is concerned with mining, reverend—

not engineering as such. Naturally, I'm sure he would be—"

Joan stopped dead, her hazel eyes as wide as they could go as she stared beyond the vicar's comfortably obese figure. He hesitated, drank a little more tea, and then began to look uneasy.

"Is—is something the matter?" he asked hesitantly.

"Don't move," Joan whispered, without moving her gaze from something beyond him. "Stay exactly as you are and the possibility is that you won't get hurt."

"I—I beg your pardon?" It was the reverend's turn to widen his eyes.

Joan did not explain further. She sat as though transfixed, watching something just beyond the immediate grounds of the residence. Where the railings of the grounds terminated there lay open country, and in the midst of this open country an object was moving and coming rapidly nearer, the sunlight reflecting from a dull grey hide.

"Upon my word, I don't understand," the vicar objected, twisting around in his chair—and at the same time he caught sight of the stupendous dinosaur which had now reached the outside of the distant railings.

"It's Herbert!" Joan cried, leaping up. "'Who'd have thought it?"

"Herbert? But I understood you to say that Herbert is a relative of yours— Great heavens, Mrs. Brooks, that thing there is a prehistoric monster, similar to the ones who invaded us two years ago—" The reverend gulped slightly. "I must depart at once, if you'll forgive me."

He snatched at his clerical hat and was through the open french windows into the grounds before Joan could stop him. When she realised what had happened, she gave a cry of dismay.

"Reverend, come back! I told you to stay here and avoid all chance of being hurt. As it is— Oh, Lor'!" Joan gasped in horror as, in racing for the rear end of the grounds where lay the gate to the main roadway, the portly vicar tripped up suddenly and fell flat on his face.

This was quite enough for the eighty-ton beast beyond the railings. It had been watching the fleeing figure intently: now the behemoth feet smashed down the railings and the dinosaur thundered towards the shouting, screaming cleric as he struggled to his feet and strove to race onwards again. That he could never make it to the gate was obvious.

Joan flashed through the french windows and sped across the lawn. She had never run so hard since she'd won the cup in her 800-yard dash in the school sports. She moved diagonally, doing her utmost to put herself between the shouting, stumbling vicar and the onrushing brute who had evidently taken a profound dislike to him.

"Herbert!" Joan yelled, at the top of her voice. "Herbert—stop! *Stop*, I say!"

She gambled everything on the possibility that by some fluke this brute *was* Herbert, a gamble she would never have taken but for Cliff's message to her over the phone. And if she were wrong? But it was too late to think of that now, for she was straight in the path of those colossal feet. Her tiny form was all that existed between the angry dinosaur and the scurrying clerics....

But the dinosaur slowed down! It even came to a slithering stop, the enormous feet gouging trenches in the smooth grass. Shaking in every limb, Joan stared upwards, past that mighty grey-ridged chest to the vast head. The mouth was as wide as a cavern and from its red depths came ground-shaking roars, either of fury or delight. Joan did not know which. Just at that moment she felt very much inclined to faint....

CHAPTER TWO
DIVINE INTERVENTION

In the distance the worthy cleric half fell through the gateway and vanished down the highway. Joan only glanced that way in time to see him go, then she looked again at the fantastic beast standing motionless and covering half the lawn with his tremendous body.

"Herbert, it *is* you?" Joan spoke softly, forcing herself to advance a few steps.

The response was immediate. Herbert rocked his bus-sized head from side to side and bared his three rows of teeth affectionately. Joan waited, the top of her head just reaching the knees of the block-like fore-legs—then the carnivore's cranium came sweeping down to give her a gentle brush of delight. The result was that she was knocked a dozen feet.

"Stop playing rough!" she protested, getting up again, and this time the sound of her voice sent the brute into sheer ecstasy. He began prancing, the ground shaking under the impact—then he darted off on a romp of sheer high spirits. When he had finished three oak trees had been uprooted and the lawn looked like a battleground. Joan stood waiting, watching the dreamy light in the usually fierce red eyes.

"By all that's incredible, Herbert, how did you ever get out of the underworld?" she demanded. "You were left behind by nearly eight hundred miles—yet you're back again, large as life! Or rather, *larger* than life," she amended to herself.

Since Herbert could not speak and explain himself he roared instead, and the din he made caused Joan to clap her hands to her ears and keep them there until the storm was over. Then she slowly began to apprehend the difficulty of the situation, even more so when she glanced towards the roadway.

Out there, standing on top of private cars, staring from halted buses, craning their necks over the railings of the grounds, were curious men and women. Most of the people in the past years had seen prehistoric monsters during the invasion period, so a diplodocus was not new. But it was new to behold a slim girl keeping eighty tons of fury at bay and talking to it in the friendliest fashion.

"Herbert, my boy, we're in a spot," Joan said frankly, leaning against his right foreleg whilst she thought the problem out. "You're quite illegal as a pet and yet I can't hide you. Have to wait until your master comes home, that's all, and see what he says. Meantime, you'd better come round the back of the house where you won't be so conspicuous."

Gathering that this long speech was meant for him, Herbert rolled forth his tongue to give Joan a lick. Fortunately for her she saw that red carpet unfurling and dodged just in time. She had no wish to be skinned by that buzz saw of flesh. It was obvious Herbert was disappointed, but he did not repeat the action. Instead he waited, looking down at his mistress with his soup plate eyes, for all the world like some fantastic animal out of a fairy story.

"Yes, back of the house," Joan decided firmly, and at that she made her way back across the ruined lawn, calling to the beast to follow her. He did so dutifully, always taking care to place his vast feet so that they did not come anywhere near her. She for her part was now completely confident again. This *could* only be Herbert, therefore there was nothing to fear from him— not after he had evidently fought his way through eight hundred miles of underground to rejoin those whom had reared him from an egg.

At the rear of the residence there was a considerable-sized quadrangle, and it was into this space that Joan managed to direct the brute from the Jurassic Age. He did his best to grasp her meaning, and finally finished up with his mighty tail thrust inside the garage and his head looking over the top of the house itself.

"You stay here!" Joan insisted, wagging a finger. "I'll see you get some food somehow. Lord knows what, but I'll do my best."

Nodding to herself she returned into the house, to be almost immediately approached by a white-faced and utterly shattered manservant.

"Madam—Mrs. Brooks—with all due respect— May I ask what that appalling animal is doing blotting out the rear windows?"

"That's Herbert," Joan smiled. "There's absolutely nothing to be afraid of, Parkinson. He's quite harmless."

"Maybe so, ma'am." The manservant glanced agitatedly over his shoulder. "Just the same I cannot help but recall the massacre—yes, massacre—which ensued during the prehistoric invasion two years ago. With all respect, madam, I am leaving."

"But—but you can't—!"

But Parkinson did. And with him went the rest of the staff. They forgot their salaries, their clothes—everything. They simply disappeared, leaving Joan with her brow wrinkled as she gazed out towards a wall of grey visible through the rear window of the lounge.

Cliff's own introduction to Herbert's return was somewhat different. The fast helicoliner in which he flew from Scotland got him into London around nine o'clock. It was still quite light, and since the evening was perfect, he decided to walk the mile and a half to his home. This decision caused him to become a man of increasing wonder, for the nearer he came to the usually deserted regions where his home was situated, the more people and traffic he seemed to encounter. They were all moving steadily northwards. In particular Cliff noticed that everybody seemed to be armed with field glasses or telescopes.

"Hey, what goes on?" he called to an ancient village worthy as he pedalled remorselessly past on a bicycle.

"Summat queer up at the Larches," the rustic replied

mysteriously, and went on pedalling.

"Summat queer at—Eh?" Cliff came to a stop and gave a whistle. "Larches! *My* place. *Now* what?"

He did not waste any more time conjecturing. Instead he abandoned the roadway and took a short cut across the fields, finding himself once again plunging through the midst of hundreds of men, women, and children, all apparently going in the same direction as himself.

When at last he came within sight of his home, he found it surrounded by a sea of people—and almost immediately he realised why. For, looking between the tall chimney breasts there was the biggest animal head in creation, two red eyes the size of soup plates surveying the shouting, gesticulating crowd as it ebbed and flowed round the grounds of the residence.

"Herbert!" Cliff gasped. "Oh, my gosh!"

Now he faced the problem of fighting his way into his own home. It demanded a good deal of physical violence and high words, but at last something resembling Clifford Brooks did reel into the lounge and look hopefully around him for an armchair.

"Cliff!" Joan came hurrying over to him. "Thank heaven you've got back! I'm getting myself all tangled up trying to explain away this situation. Herbert's returned!"

"No!" Cliff looked up dully—then he realised that Joan was not alone. A police inspector and sergeant were present, obviously apprehensive but exhibiting very tight upper lips.

"I've tried to tell them Herbert isn't dangerous,"

Joan continued worriedly. "For some reason they won't believe it."

"Our interest," said the inspector, "concerns the community at large, and the law says that the harbouring of a dangerous animal isn't allowed. If that monster in the back there isn't dangerous, I don't know what is."

"What do you propose doing?" Cliff asked bitterly. "Putting a dog collar round his neck and leading him away?"

"This is no time for sarcasm, sir. That brute will be taken away all right, though maybe not in the way you suggest."

"I hardly thought that would be the right method," Cliff admitted; then he got to his feet again and pushed back his dishevelled hair. "Look here, inspector, that dinosaur is actually a personal pet of ours and we don't intend—"

"Sorry, sir, I'm an officer of the law. The dinosaur has got to be taken to an open space and there destroyed. Like as not you know that only bombs can kill a brute of that size—hence an open space. Get bombs near property and you might blow that up as well."

"A brilliant deduction," Cliff observed sourly. "And I'm telling you that if the law dares touch that creature, I'll bring an action. You can't go around destroying people's dogs—so why their dinosaurs?"

"They get destroyed and quick if they're dangerous— and that's the issue at the moment—"

Cliff would probably have said a good deal more in defence of the dumb brute looking forlornly between the chimney breasts, but events went against him. The people who had been outside the residence grounds had become emboldened by the approach of twilight, and were now in the grounds themselves. Which was why little Albert, son of a local fishmonger, happened to be near enough to Herbert to touch him.

Only Albert was not content with just this. He wanted to be able to tell the other lads of the district that he'd actually kicked a dinosaur and got away with it.... So he kicked Herbert good and hard on the leg—but he *didn't* get away with it.

In that instant Herbert, already impatient and ragingly hungry, retaliated. He hardly felt the kick delivered at him, but he *did* know it was not a kindly act. So the foot that had been kicked rose swiftly and then crashed down again with the impact of a trip-hammer. Little Albert ceased to take an interest in the proceedings, and indeed, it would have been difficult to distinguish him from the mangled concrete of the quadrangle itself.

Definitely Herbert had had enough. Like a horse becoming restive in its stable and lashing out at the boards before and behind it, so Herbert felt penned in, desperately hungry, and at the mercy of ruthless humans, all of whom save the two he loved were out to kill him.

His fury spilled over. Into the twilight blasted the awful battle roar of a diplodocus on the warpath. He surged and swung and kicked. Half of the wall of the lounge crashed inwards and the ceiling sagged dangerously, quickly smothering Cliff, Joan, and the two police officers in plaster and dust. In the twilight they had a vision of that mighty grey wall heaving and twisting—then it had gone as Herbert got on the move.

Roaring with terrifying power he tramped through the midst of the garage and reduced it to rubble—then he charged onwards through the grounds. A sea of screaming, inquisitive humans divided before him, but not all got away. Those who did not were obliterated as utterly as if they'd been between the plates of an hydraulic press. And Herbert thundered on—hungry, furious, and disillusioned. Those two whom he had trusted had not been able to stand by him as in former times. He was one alone against the bombs and destruction of the little people. Since his doom was inevitable, there was no reason why he should not make his presence felt first. So he crashed onwards... towards London.

The telephone wires were already singing, however. In a haze of plaster dust the local police inspector bawled orders and warnings from the Brooks residence.

"Have the militia and air force commanders told immediately!" Cliff and Joan heard him saying. "Every possible method has got to be used to nail down that brute and finish him. He seems more savage than any of those we had to deal with during the invasion. *Get* him at all costs—and warn London immediately."

The telephone cradle jumped as the inspector slammed the instrument back upon it; then he returned into the half-smashed lounge and glanced towards Cliff and Joan.

"Everything's under control," he announced briefly. "By midnight that monster will have been located and wiped out. Come on, Ainsworth, we've work to do."

"Right, sir!" The sergeant followed his superior through the sagging french windows: then for a time everything seemed deadly quiet. Even the grounds had magically emptied of people now the diplodocus was abroad in the gathering night.

"For heaven's sake have Parkinson bring me something to eat," Cliff growled, settling in the dust-caked armchair. "I've had nothing since I left Scotland."

"I'll get it," Joan said, fiddling with the standard lamp until at last it glowed forth. "The staff's gone. Herbert scared the daylights out of them—including the vicar. His request for a sizeable sub to the church annexe was nipped in the bud."

"One good job, anyway," Cliff grunted.

"The possibility exists, though, that he'll sue us for damages. Herbert chased after him, and the last I saw of our reverend friend he was cartwheeling over the gate into the road. I'm afraid we've started something—"

Joan fled to the still intact kitchen regions, and Cliff gave a moody glance towards the shattered wall and broken ceiling.

"Started something?" he repeated. "That must be the king of all understatements!"

Presently Joan returned with hastily prepared sandwiches and hot coffee. She put the tray down on the nearby occasional table and seated herself to commence operations.

"No doubt but what he is Herbert, I suppose?" Cliff asked, as coffee was handed to him.

"No doubt whatever. He charged around like a friendly Saint Bernard when I called him by name. Anyway, how else do you suppose I wangled him into the quad. Good job you warned me about Herbert in that phone call from Scotland, otherwise I wouldn't have been so courageous when he turned up."

"The mystery is: how the devil did he *do* it?" Cliff muttered, frowning over his coffee. "I gave him up for lost long ago. You remember the circumstances in which we last saw him."

"I remember. The rocks fell between him and us as the borer drove homewards.... The only explanation is that his strength finally proved sufficient to smashing the rocks down. After that he must have followed the same route as our borer took and eventually he emerged."

"To the accompaniment of Scottish earth tremors as he possibly smashed away foundations. Yes, it's possible, particularly as he can survive for such a long time without food when under stress. For him to find his way right to *here* though, beats me! We're not even in the same home we had in his 'cub' or 'pup' days, or whatever you call them."

Joan reflected, a sandwich poised. "As to that, we couldn't understand how he followed us right down into the thousand-mile shaft as he did—but the fact remains he managed it. Perhaps to him we smell."

"Eh?" Cliff stared in surprise.

"I mean, maybe we give off a particular scent, or something, which Herbert can detect and attach to us. He always seems to be sniffing the breeze when choosing his direction. We don't really know the reactions of a dinosaur's brain. Fact remains that, homing instinct or smells notwithstanding, he found his way back to us."

"Yes, and now what?" Cliff asked grimly. "Every damned plane and soldier in the country has been alerted again, and I wouldn't give a red cent for Herbert's chances against that sort of opposition. What do *we* do about it? Nothing!"

"Nothing much we *can* do, Cliff, and you know it. Everybody is against us. We're considered crazy to have a sentimental regard for a diplodocus. 'Herby' will have to take his chance, I'm afraid, fond though we are of him."

To which Cliff could do nothing but agree, knowing as he did that the law was ranged against him, and that it took a dim view of an eighty-ton monster as a pet. Besides, Herbert as a pet might be very expensive. In frisky moments he might easily bring the house down, as witness the half-shattered lounge existing right now.... So Cliff went on slowly with his sandwiches and coffee and wondered how the giant of the Jurassic Age was faring.

Not at all badly, as a matter of fact. Obviously

Herbert was not a genius amongst animals, but at least he had the prehistoric advantage of being far more cunning than his latter-day descendants. He had come from a time where all instincts had been keyed up to circumvent danger, in no matter what form. This instinct had preserved Herbert when, by day, he had chosen to sleep as far below surface level as possible. It came to his rescue again now as it dawned upon his muscle-bound brain that humans might not attack him violently in a city for fear of hurting their own kind. Down underground in a city, the chances of attack were even more minimised—and Herbert knew full well that only the bombs of humans could really worry him. Bullets were nothing more than peas against his ironclad hide.

So that night, after emptying three farms of cattle on the way, he descended upon the metropolis from the north. He was not so ill-humoured now, however, since his vast belly was well lined with three cows, two bulls, and about six dozen chickens. He felt much more kindly towards human beings and less inclined to stamp on them when they got in his way.

Just the same, a monster the size of a diplodocus cannot suddenly appear in the region of Hampstead—for this was the northern point from which Herbert made his grand entrance on London—without somebody getting hurt. True, it was two in the morning and most people had gone to bed—but even then Herbert was a little careless with his feet, and left a trail across the vast array of recently laid out housing estates.

Wherever he trod, somebody suffered, so inevitably death and ruin followed in the trail of the ambling animal-mountain.

London had, of course, already been alerted for just such a happening. Accordingly, the secret sirens that had been installed just in case of war with Mars had a premature workout.... Throughout the night the wailing disturbed sleepers and set them wondering, unless they were lucky enough to hear amplified voices from police cars warning them that a dinosaur was on the loose and likely to wreak havoc at any moment.

Your average citizen is pretty stolid, though, particularly when he has survived a similar experience—as indeed all London had in the days of the great prehistoric invasion, when not only diplodoci but *every* type of dinosaur and flying horror had been at large. After that, what did one lonely brute matter?

So Herbert lumbered on, sniffing the breeze, putting his feet into buildings, wading through the remains of broken bridges, scenting all the time for something that reminded him of his beloved underworld. He found it at St. John's Wood and crashed down into the depths.

The results of this precipitate descent were cataclysmic. Naturally Herbert did not use the escalator. He simply waded towards the great elevator entrance, set the station staff flying for its life, and then he stepped into the elevator shaft and fell some three hundred feet to the enormous station proper. At that hour in the morning there were few people about—and those who were about were not present for long.

Dazed and bruised, Herbert floundered up again and then finally lumbered on to the main underground line. The live rail tickled a good deal and the sparks bothered him, but otherwise all was well. Everything smelled dank, and being underground was what he wanted. Not much chance of attack down here, surely?

This assumption was correct, insofar that to attack with bombs here would bring the underground crashing. But something had got to be done to shift an eighty-ton monster which had short-circuited nearly all the Underground system and destroyed one of the main Tube lines into the city's heart. Nothing else for it but the militia once again, and with the coming of daylight, the newspapers and radio and television carried all the details. It was one of those cases where the move against the enemy could be announced beforehand, since the enemy could not read!

Gloomily, Cliff and Joan read over breakfast of the War Office intentions.

DINOSAUR RUNS AMOK IN LONDON!

During the early hours of this morning a dinosaur, since classified by experts as *Diplodocus Carneigii*, crashed down the elevator shaft into St. John's Wood Underground Station. Loss of life has been relatively small, though several railway officials have been treated for shock. The monster, obviously one that has been in hiding since the prehistoric invasion two years ago, is now in the tunnels of the Underground, and the War Office has decided to temporarily close the entire Tube system and infiltrate shock troops into the area. It has been decided to use small atomic bombs to deal with this ferocious beast. Meantime, unavoidable delay in travel will be caused in the city due to the suspension of Underground traffic.

"Poor old Herbert!" Cliff sighed, tossing down the newspaper. "He'll never get out of this one! And I'll be damned if I still don't feel pretty rotten about it all. Just as though I'd deserted him in his hour of need. Remembering how he saved us in *our* hour of need, it's making my conscience twinge more than somewhat!"

Joan hesitated over saying something. Plainly she was worried, yet unable for obvious reasons to get to grips with the problem. Saving a dinosaur is not the kind of thing one does every day. Indeed, there hardly seemed to be a reasonable point at which to start a "Save Herbert!" campaign.... Then as Joan sat with her brow crinkled, the front door bell rang. She took no notice.

"I'll get it," Cliff said finally. "Evidently you've forgotten we have servants no longer!"

"Great Scott, so I had! Can't think why I should since I had to cook the breakfast for a change—"

Cliff hurried out of the breakfast room—to return at a far slower pace with the rubicund, portly Reverend Grimsby Maxwell toddling in front of him.

"Good morning, dear lady, good morning!" The reverend came forward with hand extended as Joan smiled weakly. "No, no, don't get up. This little matter will not take very long— Naturally it is urgent, otherwise I would not be here at so early an hour."

"How much?" Cliff asked politely.

"How much?" The reverend looked puzzled. "I confess to some bewilderment, Mr. Brooks. This is not a matter of money, if that is what you mean."

"No? I thought you'd called about the church annexe."

"For the moment that can wait. Times are not normal with the dinosaur on the prowl. I am here to ask what we are going to do about him!"

Cliff and Joan exchanged glances, then Cliff brought up a chair and motioned to it.

"Have a seat, reverend. Care for some coffee? Some bacon, maybe? Egg? Or maybe—"

"No, no, really. I have already dined fulsomely on wheaten bread, a favourite breakfast of mine. Besides, time is pressing. The War Office has decided to destroy this dinosaur."

"So we've been reading," Joan acknowledged.

"That," the reverend said, "must not be tolerated!"

Cliff blinked slightly. "But I just don't understand, reverend. According to my wife, you were attacked by this self same beast yesterday, and but for her intervention, would have been torn to pieces."

"Possibly I would, yes—but there is no guarantee of that. I confess I was extremely frightened, but once I had escaped into the road—and to a measurable degree of safety—I turned back to see what had happened to your good lady. I found her quite unharmed, talking to this mighty beast as though it was a pet poodle. I also remembered her saying something about 'Herbert', whom I then understood to be a relative of yours. Later she also referred to this monster as 'Herbert', so I am forced to the conclusion that, unlike his ferocious fellows who invaded us, he is actually quite harmless, his playfulness being mistaken for a savage attack."

"Meaning," Joan asked in wonder, "that you think Herbert was probably just gambolling when he chased after you?"

"Exactly, dear lady! After all, you yourself could not have expected any great harm to come to me, otherwise you would not have suggested that I sit still when you first saw the monster. I was foolish enough to run, which, I suppose, excited the beast."

"So where does this get us?" Cliff asked, frowning.

"Well now, it amounts to this." Maxwell got to his feet again, portly and serene. "I am essentially a peace-loving man, and in particular do I try to be understanding towards all God's creatures. I see in this big, lonely misfit of a prehistoric time a beast who wishes to be understood, who is fierce only because instinct makes him so, yet who responds to the kindly word of one small woman— And the lion shall lie down with the lamb."

"Uh-huh," Cliff acknowledged, his mouth slightly open.

"So then—" The reverend made a flourish. "I feel that we are neglecting our duty as Christians if we allow the senseless slaughter of this beast who is trying to be friendly towards us. True, he has caused damage and death, but not, I think, deliberately. His great size makes him unavoidably clumsy— Frankly, I believe there is far too much recourse to the engines of war and far too little to the bond of understanding. Besides, there *is* the scientific aspect."

"How so?" Joan enquired, her bacon congealing before her.

"Well, consider how useful it would be to the scientific records to have a *living* dinosaur to study. All those who came in the invasion were completely destroyed. To save this one would be both useful and charitable— Yes, the War Office must be asked to refrain from violence."

"That'll be something new for them," Cliff commented. "I can't see them doing it, either— certainly not because we ask them to, anyway. I tried last night to argue with the law, and so did my wife—"

"True, true, and I admit that you would probably make no headway. But even the War Office will heed the wishes of the Archbishop of Canterbury."

Cliff started. "*Whom*?"

"I referred this matter of Herbert to my bishop; and he in turn contacted the Archbishop. We, the spiritual guides of the community, consider man's behaviour towards a lone, defenceless beast deserving of the highest condemnation. It makes it worse when two members of the community are prepared to stand by him if only other busybodies would cease from interfering."

"Meaning my wife and I?" Cliff asked.

"Whom else? I admit that I have taken considerable liberty in this matter, but after seeing how you, Mrs. Brooks, behaved towards the monster yesterday, I am convinced you would be willing to look after him if legislation can be arranged to make him free."

"Of course!" Joan's eyes were suddenly eager.

"Splendid! In that way we would behave in the true Christian spirit, and science would be enriched by having a beast at first hand from which to check or correct prehistoric records. Now, having progressed so far, I think we cannot do better than go to London immediately and discover what the authorities are prepared to do. I remain sanguine they will be amenable: it does not pay to go against the wishes of the Church— And after all, at heart, the British people are profound animal lovers."

Possibly the genial reverend would have rambled on for quite a while longer, but to Cliff and Joan time had suddenly become most pressing. There was a chance, and a good one, of rescuing their pet—and that was all that mattered.

Within ten minutes Cliff had the car out and they were on their way to the city. It was not a long journey in any case, and it terminated at the concrete roadblocks that had been placed by the Army around St. John's Wood Underground Station. In the blaze of the summer sun soldiers in shirtsleeves were standing around. Others were in full battle kit with turkey-red faces.

"No passage through here," announced the officer in control of the barrier. "You'll have to detour through—"

"Let me see your commanding officer," Cliff broke in. I'm Clifford Brooks, and I've a thing or two to say concerning that dinosaur you've got down in the Underground."

So the preliminaries opened. The commanding officer was not present at the actual scene of operations: apparently he preferred to control everything by radio-television from Whitehall—but he emerged from his lair when informed that Cliff Brooks, his wife, and the Reverend Grimsby Maxwell wished to speak with him. Evidently the benign influence of the Archbishop had spread far enough into Whitehall to get the War Office on the move.

"It's like this," Cliff explained, when the C.O. had arrived and alighted from the Army car. "I'm prepared to take charge of this dinosaur and save you and your men the devil of a lot of trouble. You've nothing to gain by killing that brute, you know. Not only will your bombs play havoc with the Underground, but you'll also have the carcase to move afterwards."

"Or parts of it," the C.O. pointed out significantly. "That could make it easier."

"*Parts of Herbert!*" Joan cried, horrified. "Oh, how can you be so—so beastly?"

The C.O. looked at her sharply. The low angle of his uniform cap made his eyes sharp as daggers. "No soldier who does his duty is beastly, madam—with all respect. My orders—"

"Your orders as far as killing this animal are concerned have been countermanded," the reverend put in. "I have the assurance of the Archbishop of Canterbury on that."

"That's right." The C.O. looked bothered. "Frankly, padre, I'll be thrice blasted if I know what I *am* doing! I've got my plans laid and my plans ready, and now I'm told to hold my fire! *Why?* God knows what that brute is going to do if we don't finish him."

"That brute isn't going to *be* finished, and I want him," Cliff stated flatly. "Call your men off and let me handle the situation."

"Impossible, sir, without direct orders from the War Office. You can't flout authority like that!"

Cliff sighed and muttered something: then the genial Maxwell spoke:

"You stay here with your wife, Mr. Brooks. I'll go back to Whitehall and get the necessary permission— and if I can't get it, my superiors will. Rely on me! Remember: the lion shall lie down with the lamb."

"Yes, of course." Cliff tried unsuccessfully not to look vague and handed Joan back into the car. Then they sat and waited, sizzling in the heat, surrounded by sullen perspiring soldiers and massive concrete blocks.

"Herbert's awfully troublesome, isn't he?" Joan sighed.

"Same as a kid, I s'pose. You get to like it, though, as time goes on."

"Look Cliff, supposing Herbert *is* turned over to us for safekeeping, what do we do?"

"Do?" Cliff spread his hands. "Look after him, naturally!"

"But where? And with what? I seem to remember that he cost a fortune in food even when he was a baby. Heaven knows how big his appetite is now. As for housing him—well, I give up."

"I don't. We've got money, and we'll have public support, too, for our humane action—in collusion with the vicar."

"I hope you're right," Joan looked uneasy. "Some folks may think that we need certifying for keeping a pet which is known to belong to the most dangerous carnivora in the world."

Cliff became silent. Sure, there were drawbacks to keeping Herbert, but they seemed insignificant compared to the thought of him being decimated in the Underground. Then Joan chuckled to herself and came out with quite the most painful crack so far.

"Know something, Cliff? We christened Herby all wrong. He ought to be called Orpheus!"

CHAPTER THREE
FATEFUL AGREEMENT

It was two hours and blazing noon before the Reverend Grimsby Maxwell returned. He arrived in a big car with two Church dignitaries, a Cabinet Minister of high rank, and a War Office official of equally high rank. Never had so much high rank gathered in one spot over so remarkable an issue—to wit, one dinosaur.

"It's all right," Maxwell exclaimed, beaming upon Cliff and Joan as they struggled stiffly from their car. "We have the necessary permission for Herbert to be left unmolested, granting you both undertake to keep and control him."

"The task," the C.O. said bitterly, "will be to *get* him! We don't even know exactly where he is."

"Then find him!" ordered the War Office brass hat, as simply as that.

The C.O. obeyed—and so did his men. Suddenly there was a tremendous surge of activity around the entrance to St. John's Wood Station. Men loaded with everything except the kitchen sink tramped forward through the blistering noonday and then began the descent into the ruined elevator shaft. After that radio contact was established with the underworld and Cliff and Joan stood by to hear what was going on. The War Office official and the Cabinet Minister conversed in low tones. The Church dignitaries stood with hands behind them and stomachs outthrust as the smiling Reverend Maxwell murmured with them upon matters highly ecclesiastical.

But there was nothing ecclesiastical in the depths. The soldiers were frightened, sweating, and furious, never knowing when they'd suddenly see that eighty-ton monster before them. The whole unit would have preferred facing bombs any time.

"No sign of the damned brute," one of them growled, operating the mobile searchlight. "Might be anywhere under London, come to think of it."

Which was true. Released in the underworld, Herbert had the entire Tube network to choose from. There was the sinister possibility that a search had commenced which might go on forever.

Up above, Cliff and Joan waited. Around one o'clock they parted company, Joan heading for the nearest restaurant, whilst Cliff remained to see if anything happened. Nothing did. Joan came back at 1:45 to find things exactly as they had been.

"I wonder," the C.O. said tautly, restraining his language with the Church so close at hand, "how long these fellows are likely to be? Gets irksome waiting."

"I am sure all will be well in good time," the Reverend Maxwell observed, beaming. "It is not for us humans to try and hurry things, you know."

"Umph!" the C.O. acknowledged, or something like it, but to Cliff he added: "If there's no blasted action in the next ten minutes, I'm going down myself and ginger things up! I'll soon—"

"Hello!" bawled the loudspeaker. "Sergeant Grant reporting."

"Carry on!" the C.O. ordered.

"Dinosaur 'as been located, sir, and pinpointed on our map of operations."

"Good! Get the chains round him and the winches can do the rest."

"We did, sir. The chains broke and the winches overturned. Two men got hurt, not very badly. What do I do next?"

The C.O. reflected. In any normal battle sense he would have known exactly what to do—but this was different. There was an obstinate dinosaur down there.

"Hinstructions awaited, sir," came the sergeant's strangled voice.

"Damnit, sergeant, give me time to think, can't you!" The C.O. glanced an apology towards the Churchmen. "Can't you—can't you *reason* with the animal?"

"Reason with a perishin' *dinosaur*? That isn't in the of duty, sir."

"Mmmm, no. I suppose not. Bad show— Now let me think—"

Suddenly from the speaker there came an avalanche of best Army language followed by screams and thunderous concussions. The party around the loudspeaker stared fixedly—then they caught the sergeant's fading voice as he obviously ran for his life.

"Run for it, you men! The brute's after us—" He probably said more, but the mighty roaring of Herbert himself drowned everything else out.

"This is bad," the C.O. panted, mopping his face. "The brute has broken loose! He'll kill those men of mine—"

"No he won't," Joan said abruptly. "Here—give me that mike!"

She took hold of it and called sharply: "Herbert, *Herbert*! Stay right where you are!"

Even as she spoke, she could hear her own voice echoing through the loudspeaker connected with the underground. At the same time the frightful roars of Herbert quietened a little, and then gradually they changed to queer, half-whining noises.

"You stay right there and be a good boy!" Joan commanded. "Don't move until I tell you!"

With that she put the microphone down and dusted her hands. The Churchmen, Cabinet Minister and War Office high-up looked at her blankly.

"It's having the knack," Cliff explained, shrugging. "Herby does as I tell him, too, only sometimes I have to administer a little persuasion on the backside. Not so Joan: she's got the woman's touch."

"Amazing!" commented the Archbishop, staring.

"We're going down there," Joan said resolutely. "Come on!" She swung into the station opening and Cliff followed quickly after her. The C.O. also kept track of them, not from personal inclination but because he was in charge. Before descent could be made into the depths, however, there spewed forth a disorganised rabble of men, their faces wet with exertion, their kit half gone.

"Halt!" the C.O. roared. "What the devil's the meaning of this? Running away under fire, eh? Get back down there and make it quick!"

The men hesitated and looked at one another. Then Sergeant Grant came into view—filthy, dishevelled, and plain scared.

"This isn't in the line of duty, sir!" he objected. "I'm not going back down there with that monster, an' I refuse to order my men to do it, either."

"I'll break you for this, sergeant," the C.O. vowed. "And what kind of men are you, anyway? A woman leads the way and you lily-whites stand around and do nothing but shiver and sweat! You make me *sick! Now get below!* The little lady may need help."

Growling among themselves, the men began to follow after Joan as she began to pick her way down the crumbled sides of the elevator shaft. Rough Army ladders had been slung here and there, and by their aid, with Cliff's assistance at intervals, she completed the descent successfully. Not that such a feat was anything novel to her: she had risked far more dangerous exploits a thousand miles down in the earth.

"Now," she said, when the search-lighted underground chaos had been reached, "where is he? If you don't know, tell me where the loudspeaker unit is. He won't be far from that."

"There he is!" the C.O. cried abruptly, pointing. "My God! Look at the size of him!"

"What did I tell you?" the sergeant growled.

Joan summed up the situation, and in her light summer costume, now ruined with tears and dirt, she cut an incongruous figure amidst the burly Army men. Silent, she looked at Herbert. He was squatting on his rear legs, perhaps three hundred yards away and gazing forlornly around him. Now and again he licked his chops and growled reverberatingly to himself.

"He's hungry," Joan announced unthinkingly, at which the soldiers exchanged pop-eyed glances.

"Now you men, get ready," the C.O. instructed. "We'll have to try again with the chains and winches and—"

"That won't do any good," Joan interrupted. "It was undoubtedly your efforts to chain him which enraged him. He doesn't like to be interfered with. Just leave this to me and I'll get him to the surface."

"*You* will, ma'am?" the sergeant exclaimed. "Blimey!"

"It's not difficult," Cliff assured him. "Just a matter of feminine technique."

The soldiers quietened, but at the same time they were ready to run for it if need be. That would be their only course if Herbert flew off the handle. They were too far from the bombs to use them, and they well knew that ordinary guns would not be any use.... So they watched Joan's slim figure as she walked with the easy grace of a mannequin into the searchlight glare, each step taking her nearer to the satanic monstrosity who sat watching her with his gleaming ruby eyes.

At last she was within a couple of feet of him, a mere doll before a wall of grey. The soldiers shifted uneasily. The C.O. mopped his face vigorously. Cliff watched, but not with any trepidation.

"Herby, follow me!" Joan's voice was clear and decisive. "And mind where you're stepping! Don't you dare stamp on any of these soldiers."

Herbert whimpered and stood up. The size of him seemed even more enormous now. The ridge of his back nearly touched the rocky ceiling of this cavern through which the railway had formerly passed.

"Come on!" Joan insisted. "Follow me, there's a good boy."

Without any fear she began to return towards the soldiers, and the incredible bulk of the diplodocus followed meekly behind her. The soldiers were on the verge of running, but inherent Army training held them fast. So they crouched back against the wall of the shaft as Herbert came ever nearer them. At last he was alongside them, his legs spread like grey telegraph poles, the claws on his feet extended ready for instant action if need be. And *what* claws! They more resembled barbed hooks of four feet length!

"Up you get!" Joan ordered, administering a slap on the leg nearest to her. "Come on! No shirking!"

Herbert bellowed. Actually it was in delight, but to the soldiers and C.O. it sounded like the crack of doom.... Then Herbert began climbing steadily, tearing down rock and earth with his gross body, but none the less moving higher after each effort. Joan watched him dispassionately in the searchlight glare until his enormous tail was alongside her. Then she quickly sat on it and dug her hands into the loose folds of the scaly skin. Wide-eyed, the soldiers watched her taking a free ride to the surface.

The men of the Church, the Cabinet Minister, and the War Office high-up were all at the entrance to the station, waiting expectantly, when Herbert appeared. Naturally his stupendous head came first, flinging rockery and earth in all directions. The men scattered in alarm, wondering when that gigantic cranium was going to cease rising. When at last it did so all of Herbert was in view—and the top of the station roof had been smashed in pieces, the space being too small to accommodate him.

"Bless my soul!" the Archbishop whispered, holding his ground manfully and staring upwards.

"Quite one of the Almighty's largest creations," the Reverend Maxwell commented. "Fearsome, ugly—yet possessed of a life which it is not our duty to take—"

Nobody spoke. Maxwell froze uncomfortably. The red eyes of Herbert were looking down upon him and the cavernous nostrils were twitching. It was plain Herbert was remembering this rotund gentleman from a previous occasion....

Then down came Herbert's head and something as large as a red carpet flashed from his jaws. The reverend gave a yell of horror, and at the same moment the red, fleshy mass hit him and bowled him over. Disgusted, his face sticky with animal saliva, he struggled to his feet again, the Archbishop and second Church dignitary helping him up.

"There's nothing to worry over, reverend," Joan explained cheerfully, coming up from the rear. "Herby has taken to you. I admit his kiss is a bit overpowering, but at least the spirit is there. You know, I think he has a kind of sixth sense. He sort of knows that you've engineered his release and that is his way of showing gratitude!"

"Oh, that's it?" The cleric wiped his face. "A gratifying if rather damp performance—"

"And what happens now?" the War Office official asked pompously, keeping well clear of the huge feet. "Shall I have tanks drag the brute to wherever you want him, Mr. Brooks?"

"Ask the wife," Cliff suggested. "She's more control over Herby than I have."

Joan put her hands on her hips and glared. "Why do you Army men always have to think of dragging things to pieces or else blowing them up? You don't fasten your dog to a car and rip him to bits when you take him somewhere, do you? Herby is quite capable of walking home—and he shall! There *is* one thing, though, that you'd better do."

"Name it!" the W.O. official said promptly.

"Contact the Air Ministry and tell them to either put a hangar at our disposal close to our home—or else have one built on the spare land at the rear. Herbert will use it as a kind of dog kennel."

"I'll see to it," the official promised, at which Joan nodded, and then turned to the Church officials. "To you gentlemen I express my sincerest thanks for all you've done. I'm sure Herbert will repay your generosity one day, though at the moment I obviously cannot think in what way."

"For us," the Archbishop said indulgently, "there is the emotional satisfaction of having acted in a truly Christian spirit to this poor, dumb relic of a forgotten age."

The poor, dumb relic turned his saucer eyes and looked at the Archbishop pensively—then Joan's voice rang out.

"Herby, follow us like a good boy! And remember, watch where you're treading."

With that she nodded to the car and Cliff settled at the steering wheel. The Reverend Maxwell took his leave of the Churchmen and flopped in the car's rear; then Joan gave Herbert a final glance and settled beside Cliff. In another moment the astounding procession had started on its way—a powerful modern car, and ambling behind it the mightiest thing out of all creation....

* * * * * * *

For two days after his release Herbert did nothing else but sleep—in the quadrangle at the rear of the Brooks residence. His sleep followed a meal of four freshly-killed whole cows from the local butcher, and since it was summer and he was used to an open air life anyway, neither Joan nor Cliff had any twinges of conscience about him. Before very long he would have a home of his own: the engineers of the Air Force were already at work erecting a hangar on the adjoining field—which land Cliff had had to buy, much to his inward disgust. The cost per acre so close to London had been somewhat shattering. And so was the bill for the four cows when it came in.

"I hope," he said, on the evening of the second day, whilst Herbert still slept, "that we did the right thing."

"Course we did," Joan smiled. "The Reverend Maxwell came today and assured me of that. He convinced me that Herbert has been sent from the depths by Providence for some very special reason."

"Oh, I see." Cliff looked at his dinner moodily. "Mind you, I'm fond of old Herby, and I'm glad he's happy again, but he sure is costly. Cows, land, and the cost of repairing the lounge! It mounts up! Afraid it will go on mounting, too."

"It's worth it," Joan declared, unshaken.

Cliff reflected for a while as he ate. "The public is by no means one hundred percent behind us," he said, after a while. "One half thinks we ought to be locked up and Herbert turned into cat food; the other half praise us for being kind to dumb animals. We're even in line for the gold medal of the Dumb Friends' League. But the point is that nobody is willing to help defray the expense of *keeping* Herbert, and with an appetite like he's got, that's a depressing thought."

"What do you suggest then?" Joan spread her hands. "We can't get rid of him—nor do we want to."

"No." Cliff gave a sigh. "And I gather that dinosaurs live for hundreds, even thousands of years. I've been trying to think of some way in which he can earn his keep—such as loaning him to a film company for a thumping fee so they can make a real live film about a monster. But producers are chary of the real thing, or at any rate the actors are. Not that I blame 'em. Of course, you could go with him to keep order, only you have the house to look after. We're without staff and likely to remain so."

"There'll be a certain amount of financial return on the story we have of him for the Sunday papers," Joan commented, after consideration.

"Mmmm. Herby will eat through that in about a month, maybe. No, sweetheart, we've got to think of something useful to put him to. He's a confoundedly expensive pet."

Joan glanced fondly through the open window of the dining room. From here Herbert's tail could be seen lying like a grey lizard across the quadrangle.

"He's so sweet," she murmured. "Big though he is. We've got to keep him happy, Cliff, even if it takes all we've got."

"Sounds easy. If you saw the looks, I get at the office you might think differently—if only I could *think* of something!"

But nothing worthwhile stirred in Cliff's mind.

After all, to decide what to do with a dinosaur that will not leave you is not an everyday problem. It was not as though the animal could be used for any commonplace purpose. There were few buildings that would fit him, and certainly only two people in the whole world who wanted him—and now one of these two was commencing to wonder if even *he* wanted him.

It was the ringing of the front door bell that finally aroused Cliff from his moody speculations. He glanced up absently to discover that Joan had forestalled him. In a moment or two she returned, ushering before her an intensely clean-looking man with a very fresh-complexioned face.

"Apologies, folks, for busting in on things," he said, and it seemed somehow that he had difficulty in moderating his voice, which was singularly beery, anyway. "The name, as I told the little lady here, is Randolph K. Marsden."

"Glad to know you." Cliff got up rather tiredly and shook hands. "Maybe we'd better go along to the lounge, dear?" And he gave a significant shift of his eyes towards the looming bulk of sleeping Herbert outside.

"No reason why we shouldn't," Joan responded, with her usual devastating frankness. "Mr. Marsden certainly won't mind if he sees Herbert: he's come here especially to make a suggestion concerning him."

"Oh, you have!" Suddenly Cliff became cordiality itself. "Do have a seat, Mr. Marsden! Care for some tea, or coffee, or something?"

"Now that you mention it, I wouldn't say no to some brandy."

Cliff smiled again, not quite so cordially this time. In a few moments Randolph K. Marsden had his brandy and was spread at obvious ease in the nearby armchair.

"I own a circus," he said at last, putting down his empty glass. "Apart from owning it, I'm also the ring-master."

Cliff and Joan waited, gathering that this explained the rusty voice.

"It is hardly a top secret," Marsden continued, grinning, "that you own an educated dinosaur."

"Hardly educated," Joan corrected.

"Well, then, let's say domesticated. In plain language, a brute far removed from those other creatures which devastated us a couple of years back."

"Herbert is certainly our special pet," Cliff admitted, with a glance at that titanic sleeping bulk outside the windows. "You can see him out there, if you're interested."

Randolph K. Marsden duly looked and then became vaguely uneasy. He gave Cliff and Joan each a glance.

"Remarkably big when you're close to him, isn't he?"

"Big, and heavy," Joan confirmed. "But you were saying, Mr. Marsden—?"

"I wondered if you'd sell him to me, and if so what would be your price?"

"It would also be a pleasure for you to just take him away," Cliff smiled. "You see, he becomes something of a burden because—"

"Of his huge size," Joan cut in quickly, and gave Cliff an angry glance. "Difficult in a private way to know what to do with him, but you with a circus would be well away. Not that we'd want to part with him, though. We're extremely fond of him."

"Mmmm, I see. Well, maybe I'm wasting my time—"

"Anything but," Cliff cut in hastily. "My wife and I can probably accommodate you. Perhaps if we talked it over?"

"Could you do it now? I'm in a hurry to make up my programme arrangements. My circus opens in a week—big central London attraction. A dinosaur added to the attractions would really *be* something."

Cliff nodded, but did not dare say anything with Joan's eye upon him. Presently she jerked her head slightly, and he followed her dutifully into a further corner of the big room. Randolph K. watched them talking earnestly, gesticulating at intervals; then presently Cliff returned. He cleared his throat as a prelude to business.

"I've made it clear, Mr. Marsden, that Herbert is a very beloved pet, and that of course ups the price somewhat. However, taking everything into consideration, we're prepared to *lease* him to you for an indefinite period."

"Fair enough! And what's the price of the lease?"

Cliff hesitated, so Joan said frankly: "Five thousand pounds a week." Dead silence.

"I believe," Joan added, "that certain people loan out bent-backed horses, three-legged donkeys, and all manner of quaint pets for quite substantial sums to film and television companies—so, size for size, pound for pound, the rental is not exorbitant."

"Done!" Randolph K. said abruptly. "The price is stiff, but then you can call the tune since you possess the only known dinosaur on the face of this planet. Here's my cheque for the first month."

He struggled inside his packet, produced his cheque-book, and then scribbled busily. As he handed the cheque over he thought for a moment.

"How do we do about delivery? Won't be easy to cart a brute of that size through the middle of London. In fact, I don't think I'd be able to find a lorry big enough, or men with courage enough to do the driving."

"Delivered free of charge," Joan promised. "I'll bring him along when he's finished his snooze. Let me know the address."

"Marsden's Circus. It's a permanent circus arena in Great Walton Street. See, here's a plan of how you get there from here—"

Again Marsden scribbled industriously, and at the end of three minutes had executed a sketch. Joan took it and nodded.

"Either later this evening or tomorrow morning I'll be along," she promised. "The only thing puzzling me is: who is going to keep him under control when he's delivered?"

Marsden smiled. "We'll manage it. I have a very

capable animal trainer. He used to train elephants years ago. He'll very soon bring Herbert to heel."

Cliff's face clouded a little and he exchanged a look with Joan.

"I hope you're not implying cruelty, Mr. Marsden?"

"I wouldn't know. I never watch my trainer at work. He gets results, and that's all that interests me. Nothing to fear, though. The N.S.P.C.A. have their eye on things."

Which seemed to cover the matter. Or did it? Whether the N.S.P.C.A. had a dinosaur on their list of "creatures to be protected" was a moot point.... In fact, that was what Randolph K. was relying upon. Traditional circus animals having been phased out, he—and his legal adviser—was relying upon the fact that there was no prohibitive legislation covering dinosaurs. And before any could be created, he hoped to have already made his fortune. Whatever the issues, Randolph K. seemed satisfied enough and took his departure with more than usual haste, perhaps because the tail of the giant had started to twitch as Herbert rose at last from slumber.

By the time Cliff and Joan had returned into the dining room after seeing the circus owner safely off the premises, Herbert had floundered to his feet and was sniffing the evening air with a noise like a jet engine warming up.

"That means he's getting hungry again," Cliff commented. "Any suggestions as to what we give him? The scraps and leftovers will hardly be much use."

"I'm taking him to the circus right away, and let

them worry about it." Joan's face was resolute. "Be a good time with the twilight approaching. I thoroughly hate myself for doing this, but I'm inclined to agree with you, Cliff, that one can have too much of a good thing."

"Too much is right. Want me to come with you and give a hand?"

"Might as well. You can divert the sightseers even if you can't do much in the way of controlling Herbert."

Cliff muttered something to himself, though he knew perfectly well that Joan spoke truth. Herbert apparently had not much opinion of his own sex, but he would do anything for Joan.... Which seemed to suggest he was quite a lady's man at heart

Joan only delayed long enough to fetch her light summer coat, then she stepped out into the evening coolness and looked at that stupendous head looming far above her.

"Herbert, we're going places!" she called. "About turn!" The dinosaur, having learned the art of obedience deep in the bowels of the earth when lives had depended upon him understanding instructions, responded immediately to the command. He began moving clumsily, kneading his block-like legs up and down, until finally he had manoeuvred his head to where his rear had been. Joan watched him intently, and finally nodded in satisfaction. Cliff, watching from the french windows, spread his hands.

"Come to think of it," he said, "we could clean up a tidy extra sum if we had Marsden take you on as a trainer. 'Joanesque and her Marvellous Dinosaur,' or something like that."

"I'd even do that if I thought poor old Herby was going to be badly treated," Joan declared. "Anyway, that doesn't matter at the moment, so let's be on our way."

There was no hesitation about this, and into the main road that led to town there presently came the biggest thing on Earth, forlorn and suspicious—definitely suspicious—and beside him the two humans who still loved him enough not to sell him outright.... Inevitably men and women, and especially children, fell in at a respectful distance behind the trio, ready to flee at any moment if the giant became restive.

But Herbert was entirely docile, even if he was hungry. Not for a moment had he in mind any action that would discredit or harm his beloved mistress. He even quietly accepted being led into the circus grounds an hour later as the dusk was falling. Motionless he stood whilst Valama, the famous trainer, surveyed his new charge from a distance of fifty feet. Valama was fiery-looking, with black hair, red shirt, and tight breeches. Herbert's red eyes surveyed him impartially.

"He ees big—verra big," Valama decided presently.

"That's a habit of dinosaurs," Cliff explained.

Valama gave something like a grunt and attempted no more in his phoney Italian accent.

"Well," Joan sighed, "he's all yours, Mr. Valama. Promise me you'll treat him kindly, won't you?"

"I like the beasts. Always I treata them kindly!"

"That's just as well, because when Herby gets cross he also gets frisky—and that causes plenty of damage." Joan paused and looked up at the mighty head against the dying sunset. "Bye for now, Herby. Give mama a kiss—"

The head came down and Valama watched in fascination as that stupendous ribbon of tongue swept up Joan's face and nearly bowled her over. She smiled slightly, dabbed her cheeks and nose with her handkerchief, then turned away.

"Bye!" she called again, waving, and Cliff did likewise. "Everything's going to be fine, Herby!"

Obviously Herbert could not answer. But there was something in his red eyes as he sat forlornly watching the pair walk away, which seemed to say: "That's what *you* think!"

CHAPTER FOUR
TERROR AT THE CIRCUS

With the problem of Herbert more or less off his mind in the days that followed—believing that Randolph K. Marsden intended his 'lease' of Herbert to be more or less indefinite—Cliff felt that he could give more attention to his normal occupation, that of consulting mining engineer and specialist in geological strata. Naturally, absorbed in his work, he managed to forget all about Herbert entirely. Joan, too, had her own social activities outside the control of the household—for the servants came back once Herbert had departed—and so it appeared that everything was dropping back to the old pre-invasion era. As yet Herbert had not been billed in the circus act, possibly because his training was incomplete, and also possibly because the necessary reinforced protection around the circus ring was not yet finished. This was a trifling little item which Randolph K. had not foreseen—so, as usual when Herbert was around, the expenses department worked overtime.

Then, to Cliff, there suddenly came ominous news— and it had nothing to do with Herbert, either. Joan was the first to hear about it as they sat at dinner on an evening stifling with the heat of midsummer.

"Begins to look, Joan, as though there really *is* something in this alien invasion scare," Cliff said soberly. "You will have noticed that such a possibility has recently been dropped from broadcasting and the newspapers— That's so as not to scare the public too much."

Joan gave an incredulous smile. "But you can't mean that invasion by aliens *is* going to come about?"

"All the evidence points to it. I saw a lot of that evidence this morning, and believe me it was pretty shattering."

"*You* did? But why you? You're not a member of the government. Not even a technical adviser!"

"I am now," Cliff said. "Top and bottom of the matter is that a Government high-up who shall be nameless— because of his extremely important rank—called on me this morning, to consult me in my geological capacity. The threat of invasion and attack is so imminent that all the Governments of the world have pooled their differences for the moment and have decided to work in unison in the construction of deep shelters. And that's where I come in. I've received orders to stand by as special adviser to Government—which technically means all other Governments as well—in the matter of deep shelters. This carries a hefty retainer fee on top of the actual fees for specific information. All very nice if the issue itself were not so grim."

"This—this evidence you mentioned. What *sort* of

evidence?"

"Chiefly astronomical photographs of space machines quite close to Earth—machines positively bristling with armaments, and most of the armament alien to our science. On top of that there is absolute proof that our radar beams have tracked these space machines straight back to Mars. Remember those earlier reports of bright lights seen on the planet? Our scientists think that the aliens must have came originally from outside the solar system, and for some reason stopped off on Mars first. Maybe they were looking for something they didn't find—and now they're headed for Earth. Add to that the fact that there are dozens of authenticated cases where people have been brought face to face with beings definitely not of this world, and have been forced to answer a string of questions concerning this world, its inhabitants, and its customs."

"You mean that aliens have actually landed already?"

"One or two contingents, yes—mostly in outlying districts far from cities. Reports say they are arrogant, ruthless, and highly scientific. Where their questions were not answered freely, they used refined and excruciating torture. I tell you, Joan, in face of the records I saw today, together with photos and incontestable film and television footage, there's no doubt there's something pretty grim coming. Maybe H. G. Wells wasn't so far out when he had his vision of the *War of the Worlds*."

Joan was silent for a while, reflecting how scornful she and everybody else had been up to now over the possibility of onslaught from another world. Now it loomed right on top of her, for she knew that Cliff was not exaggerating. He had manifestly seen proofs that had convinced him, and that meant....

"Deep shelters," she mused. "And you have to design them?"

"With other engineers, of course." Cliff went on with his meal, picking at it as though he did not really care. "I have been given the rough plans, and by geologic knowledge will either veto or improve the designs. That's what comes of having made a trip a thousand miles into the Earth. Needless to state, borers similar to those that began our underworld adventure will be used again in the construction of deep shelters. The idea is to have them three to five miles down."

Joan sighed. "Makes us a lot of ostriches, doesn't it? What in heaven's name is the good of diving below? Can't we stand up and fight?"

"Against the aliens, no!" Cliff looked at her steadily. "An analysis of the weapons they have—an analysis made by ultrasonic reaction beams directed on those few space machines which have made landings—shows that they have the mastery of magnetic force and cosmic radiation, two of the most frightful destroyers known to science. Anything on the surface of the Earth—and I mean *anything*—can be volatilised completely. But several miles down we might stand a chance if lead fields happen to be well over our shelters. That's the job I've got to work out—and the sooner the better."

After which Cliff did not say any more. He had quite enough to worry over, and Joan let him be. But for her all the pleasure of living seemed suddenly to have died. The simple delight of a brilliant summer also meant nothing. Ahead was probably war more devastating than any man had ever known, war on such a diabolically scientific plane that even atomic power could only be classed as a damp squib beside it. Yet why? This was what Joan found herself wondering. What did the aliens *want* anyhow? What was wrong with their own planet that they could not be satisfied with it?

To these questions there could be no answer as yet. So Cliff flung himself into his highly secret work, and in the ensuing weeks Joan only saw him at bedtime. He had been overworked even before starting on this new project—now he was plainly heading for a nervous breakdown. But he worked on and on, throughout the scorching summer, impelled constantly by the realisation that his specialised geologic knowledge could alone provide the answers the world's Governments wished to have....

In the midst of a sultry, thundery August, the building of the first deep shelters began. Reports of aliens landing, surveying, and then taking off again were now so numerous that there could no longer be any doubt as to what was coming. And Joan, like everybody else, could only watch, wait, and hope for the best.

It came as a positive relief in the midst of this general

tension for Joan to hear of Herbert again—and it was in the form of a letter from Randolph K. Marsden himself. Apparently the mighty beast had shown himself quite tractable under the ministrations of the phoney Italian Valama, and was now ready to do his act behind the bars of a reinforced cage. Would Joan care to be present at the initial performance?

Joan did not think twice. She told Cliff over the phone of her intentions, and heard in reply that he was likely to be away for several days. Experimental work five miles down was to start immediately in a borer, the site being Aliston, a little-known region forty miles from London. As to Herbert, Cliff had so much on his mind he seemed nearly to have forgotten the dinosaur's existence.

So, feeling rather lonely, Joan set off on her own, and arrived at Marsden's Circus in ample time. The red-faced Marsden himself, resplendent in his ring-master's regalia, gave her a place of honour apart from the normal audience—in a high box near the orchestra's raised rostrum—and from here she had a perfect view of the proceedings.

"You will find him very docile and very clever, Mrs. Brooks," Marsden smiled, before taking his departure. "There are times, Valama tells me, when he seems to grieve somewhat—doubtless for you and your husband—but there it is. He'll come back to you one day when I find he is no longer good business— At the moment, though, look at this house! *Look* at it!"

Joan surveyed the tier upon tier of faces and gave an

approving nod.

"All to see Herbert, the greatest thing in show business!" Marsden exclaimed; then with a final pat to his glossy top hat he bowed himself away—to presently reappear in the centre of the ring as a spotlighted, solitary figure.

"Lay-dees and gentle-men! Welcome to Marsden's Circus—and first to the aerial thr-r-rills of the Three Theobalds!"

Having delivered himself of this tongue-twister, Marsden stalked off, and to the deafening din of 'March of the Gladiators', the Three Theobalds proceeded to do things to a flying trapeze which were nobody's business—except their own. Joan watched them absently, only half interested, her mind clouding again at the thought of imminent invasion, destruction, and the senseless slaughter of mankind. She did not smile at the clowns either, or at the knife-thrower and the strapping blonde who cheerfully risked a six-inch blade through her curvaceous body at any moment....

Then the great moment. Into view came Marsden, followed by Valama in his inevitable tight white pants. His moustachios were glistening with vaseline and two rather Edwardian curls were plastered down on the front of his forehead.

"Lay-dees and gentle-men," Marsden thundered, "we bring to you the greatest thing ever. So monstrous his size will stagger you. So huge, he only just fits within this specially-built cage. You have nothing to fear, for even Herbert's giant strength cannot snap these tungsten steel bars around the arena. Before you will presently stand a monster out of the past—a tame, quiet cousin of those savage beasts who invaded us two years ago. Here, then, mastered and trained by the Great Valama, the Most Fearless Man on Earth, comes Herbert—Diplodocus Extraordinary! Dinosaur of the Jurassic Age."

Joan watched intently. The music struck up *'Polinaise in A Major'*, and then Herbert appeared through the special entrance contrived for him. The audience stared, gasped, screamed, or yelled with laughter according to temperament. Here was something five times bigger than the biggest elephant, his sombre red eyes surveying the faces, his triple-toothed jaws yawning as though he were either hungry or tired. Probably both. Joan gazed at the mighty beast and her conscience kicked her badly. Herbert looked dejected, weary, and in an old-time colloquialism—thoroughly browned off.

Joan edged forward in her seat, putting her handbag on the broad rail of the box in front of her. Marsden, having said his piece, departed quickly and left the Great Valama in charge, and there was a look in that swarthy gentleman's eye that Joan definitely did not like. Then his whip cracked violently and Herbert began to shuffle around dismally as though wondering what exactly was expected of him.

In a moment or two it dawned on Joan that Herbert was suffering from overtraining. He had plainly been hammered, dragooned, and battered into submission, so much so that the nasty little man in the tight white pants literally had the whip hand of the situation. Joan felt herself getting hotter and hotter as she watched the beast doing its cheerful best to perform the feats demanded of it. They were not particularly original, anyway—being a glorified version of the stunts that used to be executed by elephants in bygone days. Herbert lay down, sat on his stupendous rear, knelt on two tubs, rolled over and over, played dead, and generally made an impression, chiefly because his size was so breathtaking. Then came the moment when that vast tail swung a shade too far and knocked the over-confident Valama flat on his face in the sawdust. He rose up, grinning with his teeth and glaring murder with his eyes. His whip sang and snapped around Herbert's nose, the one sensitive part of his body. He snuffled, but that was all.

Joan breathed hard and glanced instinctively about her for Marsden. Instead, to her surprise, she saw a stranger quite close to her, his hand in the act of reaching to her handbag on the box rail. It flashed upon her what had happened. The man was a common thief, and using her absorption in the act as a cover, was doing his best to make a snatch. Until Joan grabbed his wrist.

Instantly he hit at her savagely, chiefly to get free before the alarm could be raised. Joan screamed as the fist struck her violently across the face, and the man looked about him in panic. At the same instant Herbert swung round, his slow-witted brain recognising the pitch of that cry.... And, with the cataclysm of an earth-quake, Herbert was suddenly his old self and no longer the browbeaten circus performer.

He swung round violently in his own length, with the result that his huge tail again smote the phoney Italian. For the second time the Great Valama bit the sawdust— but seeing the way Herbert was now behaving, Valama remained where he was, terror-stricken, his bulging eyes fixed on those mighty front legs as they ploughed up and down.

In a word, Herbert was annoyed. He drew back slightly from facing the box where Joan was still clinging desperately to the thief's wrist—then he charged. True, the cage bars were made of tungsten steel, the strongest metal known to man, but under the terrific impact of Herbert's skull they bent sharply outwards.

There were screams from the audience and a sudden pell-mell dive for the exits in which the demoralised attendants were bowled over. Artistes at the arena entrance looked at one another, up at that mountain of living flesh, and then decided this was no evening for a performance

Joan still clung on to the thief, yelling for help at the same time. With both hands she seized his hair, ignoring his yells and frantic efforts to pull free. Then Herbert roared, rearing up on his hind legs. Real murder was those red eyes, the overspilling of hatred that he had for all these devilish people of the circus, and particularly the black-headed little fiend who had thrashed and beaten him into submission. Above all, the mistress was in distress.

Herbert charged again, and his battle cry froze the blood of the hapless men, women and children fighting to escape. The tungsten bars twanged like badly played harps. Again a mighty concussion—another resounding blow, then Herbert had smashed his head through. Joan had a brief glance of his flaming red eyes and cavernous jaws. At the same instant the blows of the man holding her dislodged her grip and she toppled backwards, hit the rail of the box, then fell into the arena below. Here she lay flat on her back, staring at a bridge of grey flesh rearing over her.

"Herbert!" she screamed frantically. *"Herbert! Stand still!"*

In the general pandemonium Herbert did not hear, or else he did not wish to. He was concentrated solely on the individual who, having failed in his bag-snatching act, was now streaking away down a side corridor, intent on getting to a window and escaping the jammed, struggling mob around the exits.... But it was not so easy as that. Herbert sensed that only a wall now separated him from his mistress's attacker—so he slammed his head into wall with all the mighty weight and strength of his eighty tons.

The timing was perfect. The thief slithered to a halt in the narrow back passage as an avalanche of bricks and plaster crashed down in front of him, to be immediately replaced by the head of the dinosaur. So much the thief a chance to see—then distended jaws that looked like the entrance to a railway tunnel flashed down upon him. The jaws closed and the huge head rocked back and forth savagely, as a terrier's might when shaking a rat.

A grisly something which had been a snatch-thief was ejected from Herbert's triple rows of teeth, and snarling, he swung around clumsily, tearing his head free of the wall and disregarding the second deluge of bricks which rained down upon him.

"*Herbert*!" The faraway scream came from somewhere underneath him, but he was not interested. He was tasting freedom again—and there was that nasty little man in the tight breeches to be attended to. The Great Valama himself realised it as Herbert swung completely round and then reared on his back legs.

"Stop him!" Valama screamed, as Joan struggled dazedly to her feet. "For God's sake, Mrs. Brooks—"

Gone was the phoney accent—and in another second gone was Valama himself. Herbert's front feet slammed down and kneaded fiercely, driving the sadistic trainer deep into the soil below the sawdust. Joan turned away, sickened, her head still whirling from the fall she had taken into the arena. She could hear the shouts of the attendants, telling her to get clear so they could fire on the maddened beast.... The noise of people fighting to escape was overwhelming.

"Herbert! Control yourself!" Holding her forehead Joan looked dizzily above her head. Herbert had evidently discovered her at last and was standing so his huge front legs formed a bridge over her. Meantime his head moved from side to side to the accompaniment of snarls that shook the circus to its foundations.

"Out!" Joan ordered weakly. "Herbert—get outside! Get away from here!"

He looked down at her, obviously realising she was not her usual practical self. Plainly it puzzled him, but that she was in distress was enough for him. His head descended, the jaws wide open. Joan swayed, but she was unafraid, knowing perfectly well that as long as he lived Herbert would never willingly hurt her.

The jaws closed, but gently, entirely around the middle of Joan's body. She was swung high into the air, clear of the confusion reigning on the ground. The sensation of swinging back and forth made her dizzier than ever, but there was nothing she could do about it.... Then Herbert advanced deliberately, carrying out the order she had given him. He strained his immense bulk against the already broken cage until the bars snapped at the base.

This was sufficient. Carrying the half-senseless Joan with all the care he could muster he smashed and floundered his way through the tiers of seats, sending the jammed, panic-stricken people into worse disorder than before. What none of them could understand was why they didn't see Joan torn to pieces before their eyes. Why such delicacy with one frail woman?

To hell went the seats. To ruin and dust went the north wall of the circus building; then Herbert was trotting gleefully in the main street, casually knocking over a couple of emergency fire engines which had been dispatched to quell the disturbance. Sirens blew, men yelled, ambulances clanged—and through them Herbert waded cheerfully, entirely satisfied with life now he was free again with his beloved mistress to protect.

Not that his beloved mistress was so happy, though. True, the cold air of the night had revived her considerably, but her sensations were ghastly. Herbert's teeth made her feel as if she was lying on a bed of nails, and every time he jolted the teeth tightened like steel. She was convinced she would carry the tooth dents to the grave.

At last, however, having survived a hail of bullets and streams of water from powerful fire hoses, Herbert was free of the struggling mobs around the circus area. He departed from the high road and ambled clumsily across the undeveloped land areas remaining from the days of devastation when his fellows had changed the landscape. Here, under the misty stars, Joan commanded that he release her.

He did, dutifully. Joan stood shivering, her clothes soaked with the moisture from his great mouth. All that she could see of him was his giant silhouette, the head cocked expectantly on one side.

"In many ways, Herby, I don't blame you for what you did," she said. "But there's going to be the most gosh awful trouble later! You killed that thief and the trainer—and the answer to that one will probably be that the law will want to kill you in return."

Herbert whimpered slightly, and that was all.

"For the time being you'd better come home," Joan sighed. "Your hangar-dog-kennel was completed only recently, so at least you'll have a roof over your head. Now follow me!"

Herbert understood the last part of the sentence if not the first, so he immediately obeyed and began to follow Joan through the summer night, alert as ever for the least sign of any danger that might threaten her.... No woman ever had a more reliable "watchdog" in tow....

* * * * * *

Meanwhile, Cliff was not having a particularly comfortable time at the Aliston shelter site. With a party of engineers—all of them Government experts—he had undertaken the command of a giant borer similar to the one in which he and Joan had once penetrated a thousand miles down. This time the trip was to be no more than five, to a point where tests had shown that there was considerable lead content.

Only the borer had jammed. It was three miles down and refused to move any further. His face grim, Cliff finally switched off the power unit and glanced at the anxious engineers seated around him in the stuffy control room.

"I don't have to tell you, boys, that we're in a spot unless we get this fault corrected," he said. "No life-boats or parachutes on a borer. The fact that we can't go forward also means we can't turn around and go backward—"

"Maybe we could climb back?" one of the engineers suggested. "Three miles isn't far."

"True, but don't forget we went through a river bed during the descent. We couldn't get past that without a machine to keep us airtight. Sooner we start looking for the cause of our trouble and rectify it, the better."

The men nodded and began to move around in readiness to follow Cliff's orders. To each man he designated a task. One was to strip the power unit, another to test the revs-per-sec. of the giant drilling screw in the vessel's nose, another to analyse the nature of the barrier before them which refused to break down, and so forth.

"And we've got to hurry," Cliff finished ominously. "Our provisions will last a week and no more. This was only intended as a preliminary investigation, remember."

The men nodded, and work began. Cliff supervised the various activities and pooled the information that he received. And the more information he got, the more worried he became—since it began to look as though the blame for the trouble attached solely to him.

"There's no doubt of one thing," commented Saunders, a mining engineer of considerable skill. "The drill's chewed to blazes. Here's a sample of the metal shards I got when I had a look outside."

Cliff looked at the twisted spirals of metal that lay in coils under the bright light. He said nothing, but immediately put them in the spectroscope equipment. The reading given made the engineers look at one another soberly.

"That's just plain steel," Saunders snapped. "I understood you to say the drill was specially case-hardened with monibendum to make it capable of standing up to the to the toughest rock!"

"So it should have been—" Cliff's face was grey. "How the devil this happened I can't imagine. Or maybe I can," he corrected. "I've been so much overworked lately I've hardly known what I've been doing. Somehow I must have forgotten to add the monibendum to the specification for the screw."

"This is a fine time to admit it," one of the men growled.

"You shut up!" Saunders told him bluntly. "I know full well that Cliff has been worked to death, and a slip-up is natural if you're at high pressure. Pity is, it had to be something so vital."

There was grim silence for a moment, three miles down in the ground. Cliff looked again at the chewed metal, then back to Saunders.

"You went outside to get these, you say. What's it like out there?"

"Hot with low humidity. Not far from a volcanic root, I'd say. Does it matter?"

"I was only wondering if there were some lucky blow hole by which we could climb back to the surface and detour around that damned river. Evidently there isn't." Silence again. Cliff rubbed his face worriedly, knowing just what the men were thinking about him. As a leader he was far too jaded mentally and physically to assume the responsibility—but Saunders wasn't.

"Only one thing for it," he said. "Radio back for an emergency borer. They'll pick us up quick enough if we leave our radio beam in operation. That will enable them to pinpoint us."

"All depending on how long they take," Cliff pointed out. "They must be reminded that before they use *their* borer they must have the drill cast in monibendum, otherwise they may jam themselves up even before we did."

"Unlikely," Saunders decided. "We've left a decided trail on the journey down since our atomic-disintegrators at the rear have volatilised the rock formations as we've ploughed through them. The path should be plain."

"Until the bed of the underground river is reached," another of the men pointed out. "After that, only a radio beam *can* do the guiding."

Saunders turned aside. "What the blazes are we doing wasting time talking! Thing to do is get the communication sent."

He switched on the radio equipment and sent out the pre-arranged call-signal. Then he waited for a response before continuing. Cliff and the other engineers waited with him, their faces tense.

Seconds passed. A shadow of a doubt passed over Saunders' rugged features.

"That's damned queer! Are they all asleep up there, or what? They *must* have received the signal. Radio waves go through rock as easily as air—"

He tried again—and again after that, then as there was still no response, he checked the instruments quickly. There was nothing apparently wrong. Juice was at full strength, since the batteries were charged by the powerful atomic motor, and even though the driving screw outside was chewed up there was definitely nothing wrong with the plant itself.

"I don't get it!" Saunders said, staring in front of him.

Nor, for that matter, did the other engineers. Nor indeed did anybody else in the world, for the failure of radio transmissions was not limited to the hapless men far down in the earth, but applied universally. At exactly midnight on this stifling August 28th, radio power failed everywhere. All over the world, all radio stations mysteriously stopped broadcasting.

Radio failure! Immediately the technicians went to work, each believing their own station was an isolated case. Then by degrees, by means of transatlantic and long-distance telephone, the truth became evident. Some mysterious power or other was completely dampening all normal radio waves.

The aliens! This was the immediate logical thought. The aliens had performed this trick by some scientific method or other as a prelude to actual invasion. And why not? What better plan than to stifle the enemy's most useful means of communication?

* * * * * * *

Of this happening Joan knew nothing. She had

gone to bed after seeing that Herbert was comfortably "bedded down" in his huge hangar. There, with straw to lie on, air conditioning, a huge water tank, and a great area filled with fresh offal—which had cost Joan a pretty penny to obtain at such short notice from the local abattoirs, Herbert was serenely happy.

Joan, too, after the excitements of the evening, and her own sundry bruises and weariness, soon fell asleep, knowing as she did that Cliff's time of return was most uncertain. When by breakfast time next morning he still had not arrived, nor sent any word, she was puzzled but by no means anxious.

Then, through the newspapers, she read of the blow that had hit civilisation. Complete failure of radio communication, and no expert had yet solved how the thing had been accomplished. Certainly it showed no signs of lifting, and the aliens were fully and roundly accused of crippling Earth's most necessary lifeline.

So important was this news, the story of the circus stampede had been forced into a minor position, for which Joan was thankful. Perhaps with this other matter to preoccupy it, the public would forget Herbert.

In point of fact the public *did* forget Herbert, because this matter of imminent invasion, forecast now by all the pundits, had become so grave a prospect—but the law, striding in impartial majesty over all everyday events, wanted to know the facts. Two men had been deliberately killed by the berserk prehistoric monster, and no less than fifty people, many of them children, had been killed or badly injured in the circus panic. So somebody had got to pay for that, and the finger was on Herbert in no uncertain manner.

By mid-morning, just as Joan was really beginning to get anxious over Cliff's non-return, the law arrived in the shape of a police inspector from the Bureau of Public Safety, and with him he brought a sergeant as witness.

"I have to inform you, Mrs. Brooks," he said, when the frosty preliminaries were over, "that the law takes a very grave view of the tragedy at Marsden's Circus last night. You are aware that a dog when it savagely bites a stranger has to be destroyed—unless there are mitigating circumstances—and therefore the penalty for causing death and mutilation amongst the public at the circus must be the—the elimination of this very dangerous dinosaur."

"Herbert is not dangerous: he was provoked!" Joan retorted. "On the one hand he had a sadistic trainer, whom he turned upon; and on the other he settled with a thief who was trying to steal my handbag. As to those in the audience who were killed, that was just unfortunate. Herbert is so big he can hardly step anywhere without crushing something. At heart he is a gentle, docile creature.

In the brief silence that followed there came a roar from the distance that sounded like a dozen lions. The inspector raised his eyebrows and gazed through the open french windows towards the hangar in the distant field.

"That would be Herbert yawning," Joan explained,

smiling weakly. "Dogs yawn noisily, you know."

"I am not interested in dogs, Mrs. Brooks—only in this dinosaur. I considered it only fair that you should have preliminary warning that the law means to take action—and quickly. I am afraid this monstrosity will have to be destroyed, despite the plea earlier put forward by the Archbishop of Canterbury."

The inspector said no more than this, but Joan knew only too well that trouble was coming. Her main concern at the moment however was not Herbert, but Cliff. Where was he? What had become of him? She spent most of the morning telephoning the various bases with which she knew he was connected, and only on the last one did she receive any satisfaction—such as it was.

Cliff had descended with a party of engineers at the Aliston Site to inspect the possibilities five miles down. Early radio messages had intimated that all was going well, but after the general failure of radio there had of course been nothing more from the depths.

"But didn't he say when he'd be surfacing again?" Joan demanded worriedly.

"He did, Mrs. Brooks," came the engineer's voice over the line. "He expected to return around four this morning, but we have had no word of him."

"Then for heaven's sake go and look for him! Since radio has failed he may be in difficulties and can't let you know. You don't just propose to sit there and wait for something to happen, do you?"

"I'm afraid it isn't up to me, Mrs. Brooks. The

Government is handling things and if there *is* an emergency they'll deal with it."

"There's one now: I can feel it!" Joan insisted. "Something has got to be done."

But for the life of her she did not know what. There was nothing the official at the other end could do, and knowing the slow-moving power of the Government, Joan realised more clearly than ever how grim the situation really was. She also knew that almost anything could happen underground. If by some chance the borer had jammed, then it was horribly possible that neither Cliff nor any of the other engineers would ever be seen again. If only radio were not so maddeningly silent!

Joan was not the only one overwhelmed by exasperation at radio failure. The engineers themselves were also victims. Every available one throughout the world was working at top pressure to solve the riddle, but by the time the early evening papers were on the streets, it was plain the radio silence was beyond the power of Earth technicians to break. The pooled opinions and conclusions were given to the newspapers and media in the form of a statement from the Government, each Government in every country using an identical technique.

Joan, dulled and frustrated by a day of anxiety both on behalf of her husband and Herbert, read the news with a sinking heart:

RADIO BLACKOUT ABSOLUTE!

Scientists and technicians, investigating the cause of radio's worldwide failure, are of the opinion that no scientific method within their knowledge can lift the "blackout" and restore communication. Tests have shown that the long wavelengths used for broadcasting are being displaced by an extremely powerful magnetic field. This means that the radio waves go forth, but due to the warp and deflection they suffer through this unexpected magnetic field, they do not reach any receiver but are instead dissipated completely.

It would appear that the magnetic field is being generated by Earth's own magnetic field, and this suggests that extremely able scientists have means at their disposal to utilise Earth's—or any planet's—magnetic field to their own advantage. The aliens would appear to be the only possible scientists who have *this* knowledge.

On that the statement ended, which was more than enough for Joan and most other people. In another part of the paper she read of the night-and-day watch being maintained by the world's observatories for signs of threatening invasion, since it was generally accepted now that radio failure was the opening gambit.

Then, in more remote parts of the paper, she came across references to action being taken concerning

Herbert; and there was also the headline:

CLIFFORD BROOKS OVERDUE!

And a brief statement, couched in Governmental secrecy, to the effect that an underground investigation he was making was giving cause for concern, as he had not returned.

So Joan acted. She went personally to Whitehall and demanded action, but though the officials were sympathetic, they did not commit themselves. One department did not know what the other was doing. Many lips were sealed. Everything was hush-hush—which resulted in a perplexed and very worried young woman leaving Whitehall fifteen minutes later and trying desperately to decide how she should act next.

Actually, though, the War Office *was* acting. They were the department concerned with the deep shelter scheme, and the sudden stepup in the apparent alien invasion was enough to make them wonder where Cliff Brooks was, and how long he would be with his shelter report. Everything was depending on shelters being built in the shortest possible time. So the order went forth to the Aliston site: "Send emergency borer immediately to investigate disappearance of Clifford Brooks and accompanying engineers."

Accordingly, the emergency borer descended into the earth by the same route as number one. Only number two did not possess a drill that was made of monibendum....

CHAPTER FIVE
CONDEMNED TO DEATH

Joan had little chance to worry much further over Cliff, for the following morning, after she had spent a more or less sleepless night, she received notification that she must appear in court that afternoon to answer the charges being brought against her and her absent husband concerning "*Diplodocus Carnegii.*" The case had apparently been rushed through due to the desire of the law to show the public that it was quick to deal with matters of social danger.

Thus ordered what to do, Joan cast around for help. She appealed first to the Reverend Grimsby Maxwell, but although he was full of sympathy for her predicament, there was little he could do. Certainly he would refer the matter to the Archbishop once again, but since the Church had already said its piece in regard to Herbert, there did not seem to be much hope from that quarter. Herbert had now transgressed the law: he had become a killer. And therefore he must die.

In face of this, Joan made the next best move and employed the most able lawyer she could find to defend her case. This was going to cost a good deal, she realised, mainly because the lawyer had to drop everything else and prepare his brief right away. By afternoon he had to be ready to take up the cudgels.

And he was. Joan sat and listened to the back-and-forth arguments in the stuffy courtroom, and wondered vaguely how men could take the time to wrangle over a Jurassic Age dinosaur when the whole world was threatened with invasion from space. It struck her very much as an interpretation of fiddling whilst Rome burned. Certainly she did not realise that the business of the world must still go on—on the legal side as much as any other—until the moment of crisis came.

And her husband? Where was he? The darkening dread in her mind concerning him made her completely disinterested in the court proceedings, and her mind wandered persistently from the legal arguments being thrashed to a finish.

"I assume, Mrs. Brooks, that the upkeep of this—er—animal is the responsibility of yourself and your husband?" the judge asked abruptly, and Joan forced herself to attention.

"Yes, my lord, he is," she assented. "And a very expensive pet he is. That's why we loaned him to the circus."

"Quite so. Your counsel has already made that fact clear. I am endeavouring to establish exact ownership of this monster, and you have provided all the verification I need. Proceed, Mr. Taylor, if you please."

Again came the legal wrangling, to which Joan had to force herself to pay attention. She did not understand the majority of the legal points raised, but the decision of the Judge was crystal clear.

"It is plain to me, Mrs. Brooks," he said gravely, "that neither you nor your husband have had any real idea of the inherent danger of harbouring a monstrosity from prehistoric times. I am well aware that pressure from ecclesiastical sources resulted in this dinosaur being given the privilege of comparative freedom, but even so, you should have known from the disasters which followed the prehistoric invasion of two years ago, that deep down this dinosaur might at any moment go berserk. I sympathise with you in your affection for this fantastic beast, but he must be removed from a civilised community. He will be destroyed tomorrow at noon, and soldiers will be specially chosen for the task."

Joan stared fixedly. "But—but, my lord, you can't destroy him! It isn't to be thought of! Why, he's—"

"He is a *danger*, madam, and that is enough. You will kindly see to it that the animal remains incarcerated in the hangar which is doing duty for him as a kennel, and I will issue the necessary orders."

There was nothing more could be said, or done. Herbert must die. Joan left the courtroom in a daze and took a taxi home. By this time she had reached the stage where she just could not think clearly. What with Herbert's doom sealed, with no news of Cliff; with threatened invasion— She sought solace in ordering three freshly killed cows, and had them delivered at the hangar. Then she went and operated the switches that opened the big doors and so allowed the ever-hungry Herbert to emerge and have an extremely belated breakfast.

In moody silence Joan lounged in the late afternoon sunlight and watched Herbert consuming his meal. He was ugly, silly, gigantic—but he trusted her and would die for her if need be. She patted the side of his great head, and he paused transiently in the midst of eating to dart his carpet of a tongue towards her in response.

"I've sold you out, Herby," she muttered, "and it'll be on my conscience for the rest of my life!"

This was not exactly accurate, but it was a good indication of how Joan felt. Actually, the cause of Herbert's troubles was the fault of Herbert himself. For a moment Joan played with the idea of turning him loose before the soldiery could arrive on the morrow and put an end to him—presumably with small atomic charges—but on second thoughts she decided against this. If he were released, Herbert would only cause more damage, then as usual he would gravitate back to his beloved mistress.

No, there was nothing that could be done—or at least, not so far as Joan could see. She finally locked Herbert up again and went back into the house. Cliff! This was the main thing on her mind now. Just as much as she was on *Cliff*'s mind as, three miles down, he and the engineers sat within the borer and plotted what they ought to do to escape.

"Without radio we don't stand a chance," one of them said flatly. "Thanks to your damned negligence,

Brooks, we've come down here in what is going to be our coffin! Why the hell didn't you remember that monibendum?"

"Never mind the recriminations," Saunders observed sourly. "Our job is to get out of here—and there's only one way. Pack all the provisions we can about ourselves and try and climb the shaft back to where we started from."

Cliff gave a weary glance. "And what about that river bed which is in the way?"

"Perhaps be a way round it. It comes to this," Saunders went on, studying the grim faces. "Either we die here as the food and drink gives out, or else we make an effort to save ourselves. We'll probably die anyway, but it's better to do it in a struggle to survive. What say the rest of you? Fortunately air is not a problem. There's plenty of that outside."

Cliff glanced towards the clock. "Half past six p.m.," he said, thinking. "I told headquarters we'd be back at four this morning, so by now it will probably have dawned on them that we're stuck. If so they'll send another borer."

"Which won't have a monibendum screw," Saunders added. "That means they'll jam down here same as we have. We might be able to stop that disaster if we get on the move. Let's be going."

The course of action decided upon there was no further hesitation. Each man loaded himself to the limit, not only with food and drink, but also with small rock-cutting tools and mountaineering equipment;

then one by one the half-dozen men went through the open airlock into the narrow rock tunnel outside. It was a tunnel entirely created by the borer itself and stretched diagonally upwards in the beams from the men's helmet lamps.

"Come on," Saunders growled. "Three miles isn't so far."

Not on the surface, certainly, but three miles *upwards* was a very different matter, as the men soon found. After the first five hundred yards it necessitated them bringing their mountaineering kit into use so they could ascend the sheer precipices that were the only way to get to the higher levels. To follow the actual course the borer had originally taken was impossible, since falls of rock had occurred behind it, and it was these that had to be negotiated.

The hardest task of all, which took them nearly three hours, was mounting a five hundred foot spur, the top of which brought them within hearing distance of the underground river they had breached on the way down. Far as they could tell, it was about a mile to the north of them.

"Here's the tough part," Saunders commented, gazing around him in the helmet lights. "Solid rock to the left—empty void to the right where the noise of that river is coming from. Where do we go from here?"

None of the men answered, because they could not. Cliff, with Saunders beside him, considered the great pinnacles—as far as they were visible in the lamplight—then he looked overhead at the roof. They were in some kind of great natural cavern and the roof was quite a hundred feet above them. Without doubt they had reached an insurmountable barrier.

"Say, do you hear something?" one of the men asked abruptly.

"Uh-huh—the river," Saunders acknowledged. "Don't forget we provided a first-class underground Niagara when we smashed through the river bed—"

"I don't mean that. Something else. Just see if you can detect it above the noise of water—"

Each man became silent, intently listening, then upon each one of them there was gradually forced the realisation that there *was* a different sound, and becoming louder, too. It was a shrill, high-pitched whining note, which as it became more intense set the teeth on edge.

"It's a borer!" Cliff exclaimed suddenly. "I'd know that sound anywhere! It's the drill grinding through rock—somewhere above. Hell, but there's going to be trouble! If they break through that cavern roof up there they'll fall nearly five hundred feet."

"No means of warning 'em, either," Saunders muttered, staring above. "The only hope is signalling with these lamps the moment the nose of that borer shows through."

The other men nodded, listening and watching, with every nerve taut. After a while the long-distance beams of their lamps showed quite clearly the showers of stones that were commencing to descend from the roof. Immediately this happened Cliff pulled off his steel helmet, removed the lamp from it, and then returned the helmet to his head. Settling on one knee for maximum steadiness, he prepared to flash a warning the moment the borer showed signs of breaking through.

This happened within five minutes. The rock fall increased noticeably, then there suddenly appeared the blurred spur of the frontal drill, spinning at thousands of revs per second, fed by a constant flow of lubricant. But Cliff's practised eye noted something about that drill. It was not running true. The rocks it had so far broken up had evidently proved too tough for it and bent it considerably out of alignment. Once again, evidently, the lack of monibendum could be blamed.

This much he had time to notice, then the actual nose of the machine began to emerge, smashing rocks down into the gulf in the process. Since the inside of the borer was mounted on universal bearings, the cabin was upright even though the outer shell was directly vertical. But within the cabin the men must have been wondering why their downward piercing searchlight was failing to reflect from any object. They were literally squeezing themselves out of the rocks into empty space.

Cliff waited until the front prismatic window of the vessel came into sight, then he signalled frantically: "STOP! YOU ARE DROPPING INTO CHASM!"

Evidently the message was immediately picked up, for the roar of the borer's atomic motor ceased, and with a whining scream the drill ceased to revolve. There was an uncanny pause for a moment, Cliff and his party separated from that metal egg with its prismatic window by a distance of a hundred feet. Then from the borer there came light signals.

"ASSUME YOU ARE GOVERNMENT PARTY LED BY BROOKS. HOW DO WE MAKE CONTACT? RADIO IS DEAD."

"DROP A ROPE," Cliff signalled back. "ONLY MEANS OF MAKING CONTACT. OUR BORER IS JAMMED FIVE HUNDRED FEET BELOW."

The signalling ceased. A second searchlight augmented the glare from above; then out of the midst of it there came whirling a long 200-foot coil of mountaineer's rope, secured at the further end through the trap in the borer's nose. After the rope had swung back and forth for a moment or two Saunders made a grab and caught it.

"Suppose," he asked, considering, "that the weight of one of us on this rope pulls the borer through the hole?"

"Unlikely," Cliff told him. "Only the nose has got through, and the middle of the machine is three times as wide as the nose and, from the look of it, firmly jammed. We've got to risk it, anyway. Not that there'll be much advantage even then, because that machine can't turn around and go back home. And even if it could turn, the screw won't last much longer."

Saunders gave a grim nod and held out the rope. "You first, Cliff. You're the leader."

"Which is why I'm going last," Cliff retorted. "Hurry up, boys. You first, Sedgwick."

Engineer Sedgwick obeyed promptly, and his strong

muscles aided him in rapidly climbing to the borer's nose-trap. After that, since the weight of one man apparently did not affect the wedged machine in any particular, the ascent of each man was swift. In ten minutes the control room was jammed with the two parties, busily shaking hands with each other.

"Didn't expect to find you so soon, or in such an unexpected place," said Evans, the leader of the second group. "What happened?"

Cliff told him. "My fault entirely for overlooking that monibendum. You know your own screw's off true, I suppose?"

"I know," Evans acknowledged bitterly. "We struck virgin rock higher up and it ate hell out of the drill—And thank God you happened to be where you could stop us falling into the chasm. Our radar equipment is somewhat on the blink, otherwise we'd have been warned in time by getting no near-echo. All part of the radio trouble, of course."

"You mean *your* radio is dead, too?" Cliff questioned, frowning.

"Every radio in the world is dead, Cliff. The aliens are back of it. A dampening wave prior to invasion. Anyway, that's beside the point at the moment. We've got to get back home, but I'm wondering how. I could probably withdraw this bore with the tractor gear, but that drill won't stand up to piercing a way back—and the route we came by fell in behind us."

"Which makes us sealed?" Cliff questioned.

"That's it."

"And the radio dead," Saunders commented. "This is one hell of a mess if you like!"

"Radio failure doesn't signify," Evans said, surprisingly. "We have contact with the surface by cable telephone. Don't forget we knew radio wouldn't work before we started down, so we put a massive drum of cable on the back of the borer and played it out as we descended. I don't think the rock falls will have smashed it anywhere. Rock never falls as level as a guillotine blade."

"Try the phone out," Cliff ordered. "I want to take a look to the rear."

Evans nodded and moved to the equipment. Cliff crossed over to the rear prismatic windows and surveyed the scene with the back searchlights. A little way to the rear there was a wall of tumbled rock, a monstrous cave-in from where borer two had passed by.

"How'd you get past the river?" Saunders asked, and Evans glanced up from operating the telephone.

"Our sonic detectors gave us ample warning of its course and position. We detoured."

"You were lucky: we went through it—"

"I'm making contact!" Evans interrupted tensely. "Hello there! Evans speaking. Are you receiving me?"

"Yes, line's okay," came the curiously remote response in the earphone.

"Thank heaven for that! We're ditched down here, nearly three miles, but let the Government know that Brooks and his party have been rescued. However, they have had no chance to make shelter exploration. See to it that another borer is sent down, to clear the track for us. We're blocked by a landfall of about—" Evans looked at the last reading on the sonic detector that automatically, by reflected sonic waves, gave the depth of the barrier. "About two hundred feet," he concluded.

"We dare not blast our way out in case everything falls in around us. Another borer might drill and—"

Evans tensed and listened, his expression changing. "There isn't another borer!" he cried. "But damnit, man— Only the two? Original and relief? Just a moment."

Evans looked at the sweating faces around him. He singled out Cliff for attention.

"Any ideas, Cliff? You've gathered the drift. There's a packed mass of rock two hundred feet thick between us and the way back—and there *could* be plenty of other falls on the upward tunnel we made, too. We can't shift this machine—yours is out of action—and we don't dare blast. There's no other borer, and to build one would take weeks. Likewise, it will take men many weeks to dig through the barrier, and until they do, food cannot reach us. Our food will last a week—no more. It has to provide for two lots of crews, remember, and the stuff you have with you won't make very much difference. We're in a spot," Evans finished, breathing hard, "and I'll be damned if I know the way out."

"There's just one chance," Cliff said slowly. "Tell them on the surface to get in touch with my wife immediately. She must be told every detail of the situation—as you've outlined it to me—and then she must get Herbert."

"Herbert!" Evans stared blankly. "You mean that hulking dinosaur you leased to Marsden's Circus?"

"The same. The strongest living creature on the face of the Earth. He'll be more useful saving us than capering around a circus—"

"He isn't doing that any more," Evans interrupted. "He went off the deep end at the circus and raised the devil—but you wouldn't know about that because you were underground."

"But he's still living, isn't he?" Cliff demanded anxiously.

"Far as I know."

"Then get him! Joan will grasp the situation and direct him as need be. He'll clear this barrier as fast as flesh and blood can do it. I *know* what he can do. Two years back he shoved a borer of this size along with his nose and thought nothing of it— Hurry it up, Evans! It's our only chance."

Immediately Evans turned back to the telephone and relayed the instructions Cliff had given him. After which there was a nerve-straining wait of nearly half an hour; then the phone buzzer burred.

"Yes?" Evans asked quickly, and he listened with a deepening frown; then he turned to Cliff. "That pet dinosaur of yours has been sentenced to death. There was a court case over him this afternoon, and your wife has been ordered to keep the animal in the hangar-kennel 'til tomorrow, when it will be destroyed."

"Give me that phone," Cliff ordered, and he whipped it up. "Now listen," he continued to the unknown at the other end of the wire, "you tell the authorities that if my wife is not permitted to use that dinosaur, twelve men are going to die entombed. Men's lives are more important than a dinosaur's! Hurry it up and ring back!"

Again a long wait; then the buzzer again. Instantly Cliff whipped the phone up.

"Well?"

"Okay, Mr. Brooks. I contacted your wife again and she got in touch with Whitehall. Since the dinosaur is the only way in which you can be saved, his sentence has been suspended for the moment. Your wife is going into action immediately!"

"Good for Joan!" Cliff cried. "Keep in touch and tell us how things go."

The responsibility for the rescue was entirely up to Joan now, and since her husband was working for the Government, she had the highest authority in the land behind her endeavours. Nor did she flag: the call to action was all she wanted. At one stroke she had secured Herbert's release once more—even if it was only to be temporary—and she also knew that Cliff was still safe.

Things moved fast. The Government ordered a special train so that Herbert could be moved in the fastest possible time to the Aliston site. By the time this was accomplished, it was the early hours of the morning and Joan was directing the mighty beast and the few men who dared to work alongside her, trusting to luck that her influence over the animal would save them from being trampled upon.

Not that Herbert had any intention of behaving badly. His mistress seemed to be in good shape, and obviously the men with her were trying to assist her—so Herbert was perfectly docile. He was shown the area where the second borer had commenced its descent, and nothing more was needed. Being thoroughly used to the underworld, Herbert began to descend into the depths, following the broad tunnel the borer had made, a tunnel only just big enough for the stupendous beast to move in. Behind him came Joan and a band of rescuers, equipped with all the necessary tackle for breaking a way through the barrier somewhere below.

Evans had been incorrect in his assumption that there had perhaps been other falls of rock in the tunnel. There were none, so in the blaze of the powerful torchlight Herbert went lower and lower into the depths, occasionally nosing a boulder out of the way, always clearing the track for the humans who came behind him. Once or twice the men with Joan wondered what would happen if Herbert went suddenly off the deep end. Down in this narrow space they would not stand a chance.

But Herbert did not go off the deep end. He was aware by now that he was needed for something important, and if that was going to make his mistress proud of him, nothing else mattered. So finally the three miles of descent were covered, and the barrier became abruptly visible. Immediately one of the men clipped in his portable telephone and made contact with the borer lying beyond this wall of virgin rock.

"They're okay, Mrs. Brooks," he announced. "In good heart and waiting for the next move. Your husband sends his love to Herby."

Joan smiled, tired though she was after being raked out of bed to perform this fantastic journey into the depths.

"Do you think," the men's leader questioned, "that this animal will be capable of breaking through a mass like that, ma'am? It's two hundred feet thick, remember, and goes up for about a hundred feet."

"If I know Herby alright, he'll do it," Joan answered confidently; then she turned to the huge beast whilst the men looked on in doubt and some fear.

"*That!*" Joan said, pointing to the rock wall. "Push it out of the way, Herby. Same as you used to down below. Break through to your master. *That! Push!*"

Herbert stood quite still for a moment or two, his slow brain absorbing everything Joan had told him, then presently his vast head turned and the red eyes surveyed the wall in the torchlight.

"Push!" Joan insisted, and administered a slap on Herbert's side to get him started.

Finally he seemed to understand, and placed the top of his head against the wall. His back legs slithered until he jammed his claws into the rocks. Then he began to strain with every ounce of his stupendous strength and eighty tons of weight. Small rocks on the outside of the barrier cracked and tumbled down, but the larger ones stood the pressure. And everything Herbert tried to do to push them away failed. Finally he ceased and stood snorting, looking down on his mistress enquiringly.

"Lift me up," she instructed, and she sat serenely in the monstrous jaws as they closed about her. Fascinated, the men below watched as she whirled up to the point she directed. Here she clambered on to the rocks and pointed to the first giant boulder nearest Herbert.

He understood. Like a living mechanical navvy his jaws closed round the boulder and lifted it in its entirety, dropping it at the base of the barrier. So Herbert's task began—to remove all the top rocks and leave just enough room for the men beyond to scramble over the barrier to safety. To the dinosaur the lifting of these mighty stones was nothing more than a game. To men it would have meant cranes, winches, and endless hours of backbreaking effort and manhandling. Slowly but surely a way was being made over the top of the barrier, Joan constantly giving directions and indicating to the willing creature which stone she required moved next.

Inevitably, it was only a question of time before the way through was absolutely clear and Joan found herself in the bear hug of Cliff's arms whilst the rest of the men surveyed the mighty beast who had freed them. They wondered if he was really half so devilish a beast as he was made out to be.

CHAPTER SIX
ALIEN INVASION

The matter of Herbert and his release of the entombed engineers was something that made the Government sit up very promptly. So did the newspapers and media—and so did the Church. The fact that he was to be condemned to death on the day following his amazing escapade below ground was something that the Government itself promptly took up, mainly through the columns of the newspapers. By breakfast time the following day, whilst Cliff and Joan were still soundly sleeping and Herbert was snoozing in his hangar, every newspaper in the country had the story, and each and every one was unanimous in the declaration that Herbert must not be destroyed at any cost.

The various headlines ran:

DINOSAUR SAVES TRAPPED ENGINEERS!
CONDEMNED MONSTER SAVES TWELVE!
HERBERT MUST BE SAVED!

In the face of which the authorities felt they dare not move to implement the law in putting Herbert into permanent sleep. On the other hand, it was argued that

Herbert had merely acted so gallantly because he had been under direction—and also it had not been a particularly heroic escapade from his point of view. He had merely utilised his giant strength, which was no hardship as far as he was concerned.

Herbert, though, had now become a major issue in the affairs of society, a fact to which Cliff and Joan presently woke up. It was also argued in the hush-hush quarters of the Government that Herbert might prove invaluable during the sinking of deep shelters. For shelters there had got to be, and quickly. With the neutralisation of all radio communication still in being the menace of invasion remained—though up to now there was no sign of visible space machines approaching from the void.

Cliff made out his report to the Government on the failure of his mission to penetrate to a likely shelter site, and was immediately ordered to stand by for further investigation the moment a new borer could be constructed with a monibendum screw. So for the time being, at least, he was back where he started and, whilst the third borer was being constructed, he continued with his normal profession of consulting mining engineer.

And Herbert? The militia did not come to destroy him. There came the old problem of keeping him fed, and the only way Joan could do this was to come to an arrangement with the abattoirs that had so far supplied the monster's needs, for them to deliver a daily supply of meat. It would be costly, but this was essential if the right thing was to be done. So Herbert was happy enough and quite unaware how close he had come to extinction. Joan saw to it that he was exercised in the field around the hangar at regular intervals, and for the rest of the time he seemed quite content to snooze in his specially built home.

Just the same, this state of affairs could not be allowed to continue. Both Joan and Cliff wanted to know definitely where they stood. The possibility that Herbert might be under the death sentence still remained an open question. So Joan, since Cliff could not spare the time, appealed through the court for a definite ruling, and behind her she once again had the massed support of the Church, led by the Archbishop and the Reverend Grimsby Maxwell, together with the N.S.P.C.A. It was monstrous, declared these august bodies—with no pun intended—that the destruction of so sagacious an animal should be contemplated just because he had 'accidentally' killed two men because of his great size. As for the stampede and death and injury caused— well, had not human beings themselves been as much to blame?

So, in camera, the court considered this plea, though it was known from the very start what the answer would be. To go against the wishes of the public, Church, and N.S.P.C.A. would be dangerous. Herbert had become a national idol all of a sudden and his depredations forgotten—except by the minority who had suffered at his 'hands'. Toy-makers were even experiencing a boom making small models of Herbert for children's enjoyment. To bump off the original would hardly be the thing.

Nevertheless, the law had to show that it had *some* authority, so in the end a compromise was worked out. Joan, present in the court by command when the decision had been reached, listened to the judge's observations—the same judge who had previously delivered condemnation.

"Let it be understood," his Lordship said, "that we have very carefully deliberated this matter, Mrs. Brooks, weighing the advantages of this dinosaur against his disadvantages. We have now arrived at the conclusion that he may at some future date be of use to the State, though in what capacity it is not for me to say. That being so, the sentence passed upon him will be rescinded, and instead he will become a State charge, as are animals drafted into the services which defend our country."

"I see," Joan said quietly, realising that she was evidently going to lose Herbert after all, though not by death.

"We have also endeavoured to take the humane view," the judge proceeded. "Not only the humane view, in fact, but the very important one that of all the people in this world who are accustomed to handling animals, only you are capable of controlling this dinosaur. That is a vital factor."

Joan nodded, wondering what was coming next. She wished his learned Lordship would speed things up a bit.

"It has been decided that—er—Herhert shall be removed from the hangar where you have housed him and become the entire responsibility of the State. For that purpose, Milford Park—a derelict area of which you may be aware in the centre of this city—will be specially prepared for him alone. It covers a considerable area and will be ideal for the monster to roam about in. Further, the public will be allowed to see him from the safe side of enclosing rails. In other words, he will become an exhibition piece until some emergency may demand he be called to action. The exact time when he will be transferred to Milford Park cannot yet be stated: that will be contingent on how quickly the area can be made ready for him. Until that time, Mrs. Brooks, the monster remains under the control of yourself and your husband."

By and large the decision was not such a bad one, as Joan realised when she came to think it out. At least it would mean she had a hand on Herbert and the expense of keeping him would be eliminated. Yes, it was not so bad after all. The only thing she doubted was that Herbert would be content to remain in an enclosure and be stared at. There was no way of assessing the strange workings of his brain.

Cliff, too, had no fault to find with the decision— so it was just a question of waiting. Meantime, events went on pretty much as they had always done, with the one exception of dead radio. Astronomers were still on the watch, and yet there was nothing to report. They even wondered amongst themselves if the aliens *were* responsible for the radio blackout. If so, why such had there been such a long delay between the first move and actual onslaught?

Not that Earth's Governments heads regretted the delay. It gave them a chance to marshal some semblance of defence, but they knew that even at its best it would not be capable of standing up to sustained attack from master-scientists. It was possible the aliens were quite aware of this, and so were not hurrying themselves in consequence.

In a fortnight the rush job put on borer number three was completed, and Cliff was once again ready for an excursion into the depths. The interval since the last disaster had given him the chance to get some rest and he was a much fitter man. Further, he was reassured by the knowledge that if trouble again ensued, Herbert could be called upon to effect a rescue. This time, as in the case of borer two, there would be constant telephonic communication with the surface. So Cliff and his party of Government engineers set off once more into the underworld—and not two hours after they had departed from the Aliston site Joan received word that the 'compound' intended for Herbert was complete. Would she be good enough to direct the beast to his new quarters?

She did so, once again feeling very mean. Each time she did a job of this nature, she felt she was deceiving Herbert to the limit, and it struck her as a shabby reward for the willing obedience he always showed. However, the job had to be done, and done it was. She did not delay too long once she had led him into the enormous enclosure—only long enough to survey the quarters where he would live, a big, once-demolished building which had now been converted to his particular uses, with water laid on. Food, presumably, would be thrown over the immensely high, triple rows of railings entirely encircling the enclosure.

"I'll come and see you often, Herby," Joan promised as she took her departure. "You're the property of the State now, and a very important fellow."

The way his red eyes looked at her in the evening sunshine she was reminded of a parrot's one-time observation: 'This is a damn fine trick, this is!' Then she went on her way and reported to the authorities that the 'transfer' had duly been completed.

Upon arrival home, she received the first news from the Aliston site. The five-mile boring expedition had proven entirely successful and her husband and his party were in good heart. They expected to have their preliminary investigations complete within two or three hours, and then the return journey would commence. So apparently, at the moment, everything in the garden was just as it should be.

But no—not quite. As night came swiftly over the Western hemisphere, the watchful astronomers of Mount Wilson in California began to find their long vigil bearing fruit. Something was happening on Mars. Immediately all astronomers were alerted, and at Mount Wilson in particular the experts gathered around the reflector screens of the vast 800-inch telescope. This instrument, though by no means the possible ultimate in telescopic devices, was nevertheless powerful enough to reveal the disc of Mars with absolute clarity. And there was no doubt that from the edge of that disc tiny spots of lights, probably the exhausts of hundreds of space machines, were flashing! Nor was the phenomenon only visible for a moment or two: it recurred at intervals throughout the night, which seemed to suggest that hundreds of space machines that had previously been on the red planet had set off on a journey to Earth.

Immediately the telephone wires sang around the world. All governments were informed, and they in turn transmitted their orders to the various defence commanders. It was quite impossible to tell at the moment, of course, when the space machines would reach Earth, since there was no indication as to their ultimate velocity. But it might only be matter of weeks. The astronomers could only stand by, ready to start computing the moment the giant telescopes had picked up the oncoming space machines.

Cliff, in the midst of returning from the depths; heard the news over the telephone, which pretty well made hay of all his underground researches. There would be no time now to get the shelters built: indeed, none of the sites had yet been thoroughly examined. The Aliston site was the only one on the list so far.

"Which means we're too late—as usual," he commented bitterly to Joan as they sat at breakfast the following morning. "Our expedition was eminently successful and we gathered all the details we needed, but to get a shelter built down there under two months would be impossible."

"Obviously," Joan admitted gloomily, looking up from the morning paper. "I see here that the astronomers predict that even at their present speed the aliens will be here in just ten days. What does the Government have to say about that?"

Cliff shrugged. "What *can* they say? They know damned well they've left it until too late. I should have been instructed to make my preliminary investigations a year ago. No reason why I could not have done, either. It was simply that nobody really believed that alien invasion was genuine, or possible."

"If it comes to that, there's no certainty of it *now*. Just because the aliens are headed for Earth does not *necessarily* mean they intend to invade. Their visit might be peaceful."

"Little use kidding ourselves, I'm afraid," Cliff said. "The blackout on radio is quite sufficient warning— Oh, let's change the subject! How's Herbert going on? Any news?"

"Apparently he's under the care of the Zoological Ministry and being given the same attention as any other wild animal. I rather thought it might be a good idea if I went and saw him each day, just to keep him up to standard. He's liable to forget all the tricks he's learned if I don't keep him refreshed—and if we find him lacking in an emergency it'll be the end of him. He's more or less on borrowed time as it is."

Cliff grinned a little. "If the aliens land and see him before they see us, they'll think they've landed in the Carboniferous Age! Anyway, it's a good idea of yours to go and keep him up to scratch. Give him my love!"

Which was exactly what Joan did. She could not help but notice, though, as day succeeded day and she paid regular visits to Herbert's enclosure, that he was not his normal self. He frisked about a good deal, but it was apparently more or less of a duty than a spontaneous reaction of delight. Just what *was* the matter with him Joan did not know, and there was no veterinary surgeon with sufficient courage to make a diagnosis. So Joan had to figure it out for herself.

It could not be because he was lonely, for every day hundreds of spectators came to view him, and as far as possible behind three rows of railings, the centremost one electrified in case he went berserk, he did his utmost to make friends. Nor could it be that he was grieving because of separation from Joan and Cliff, for when they had owned him he had always been a mile away in his hangar, and their visits—Joan's anyway—had been no more numerous than now.

Was it perhaps the absence of nitrogene gas in the atmosphere, which, prevalent in the Jurassic Age from which Herbert had come, had been mainly responsible for the monster's longevity? This was certainly a possibility, but nothing more. The one factor against it was that Herbert had been unaffected up to now and had deliberately come back to the upper world from the lower—which instinct would not have allowed him to do if it would have meant his death.

Altogether it was a puzzle to Joan, the only person who really made an endeavour to solve the mystery. Then on one of the days as she was leaving Herbert the truth dawned upon her, as though there had been some mystical communication between herself and the mighty beast who was so devoted to her.

"I believe," she told Cliff that evening, "that what he wants is a mate! Only natural when you come to think of it. How would *you* like it to be absolutely the one surviving specimen of your race amongst a lot of strangers? You'd want somebody to keep you company, wouldn't you?"

"Uh-huh," Cliff grinned. "Preferably female."

"Very well then. Put yourself in the position of Herbert."

"That's somewhat difficult, but I see what you mean and I think you're right. Time we remembered he's a big boy now. But there's nothing we can do about it, so I'm afraid he'll just have to go on moping."

"Well, to my mind—" Joan started to say, then she broke off in sudden frozen anticipation as upon the stillness of the summer evening air there came a whining from the not-too-distant city. The rising and falling wail of sirens, presently augmented by others in the immediate neighbourhood.

Cliff got to his feet. "This sounds like it!" he announced grimly. "I happen to know that the Government order was for the sirens to be sounded only if actual invasion were imminent. It looks as though those aliens crossed space quicker than was expected."

He strode to the open french windows and looked out on to the calm of the summer evening. Overhead the sky was misty blue. In the direction of London heavy clouds had gathered, as though a thunderstorm were imminent. Everything was sultry, still, and filled with a definite foreboding. But as yet there was no hint as to why the sirens were sounding.

"Anything doing?" Joan came quickly to Cliff's side and looked out on to the calmness, way beyond Herbert's deserted hangar and out to the misty meadow behind it.

"Not yet. But they wouldn't sound the sirens for nothing. I'll see if I can get any news."

Cliff turned and crossed quickly to the telephone. In a moment or two he had the War Ministry's special department on the line.

"What's the matter?" he inquired of Margetson, whom he knew very well. "This a siren rehearsal or the real thing?"

"Real thing, Cliff—unfortunately. We've had the tip-off from Mount Wilson that space machines are descending towards Earth from four separate directions. There appear to be several hundreds of them. Naturally, the governments of the advanced countries fired off guided missiles to destroy them whilst they were still in the upper atmosphere, but the craft are protected by some kind of force field that completely negated even atomic blasts! Reports since then have said that several have already dropped in Europe and some are even on the coast of France, which makes it a logical bet that they'll head this way. The damnable thing is that there's no radio with which to give anybody instructions. Have to hope for the best."

"And a meagre hope that is!" Cliff retorted, ringing off.

Joan turned to him quickly as he came back to her side.

"Bad," he said bluntly. "This is the real thing—"

He broke off, staring with Joan as out of the misty sky, perhaps two miles away, there suddenly streaked something like a gigantic meteor. The only difference lay in the fact that its speed was slowing down as it moved, which would not have happened with a genuine meteor. It vanished over the horizon, but there was no following concussion. Hardly had it disappeared than there came another—and another—all apparently dropping close to the same point.

"Spaceships?" Joan asked, with a quick glance.

"'Fraid so. That glare around them is either from a magnetic or electrical shell with which they're protecting themselves, or else it's from the jet exhausts. The fact remains we're now squarely in it and God knows what happens next!"

The answer to this one came rapidly—not just to Cliff and Joan, but to everybody in the world. Until midnight, as far as G.M.T. was concerned, the shoals of alien space machines cleaved down from the upper atmosphere and landed at points always distant from a city or town. Evidently the aliens did not choose to immediately land in the midst of a community, and the probable reason for this was that they wished to avoid an immediate conflict with city defences.

Instead, after the last of the landings had ceased— and in this time observers throughout the world had counted some five thousand space machines in all— there came a brief lull. But when the total darkness had closed down, at least over the Western hemisphere, the aliens went to work in earnest.

First, their magnetic and electrical-dampening instruments blotted out all lights everywhere. In the space of ten minutes, as a hundred alien machines swept back and forth over London, every light in the city expired. The powerhouses worked as usual, but their energy generation came to nothing. How the trick was done nobody knew, but the scientific ones assumed that the aliens had the secret of altering light-wave vibration, by which the vibrations were no longer visible to the eye. This did not preclude the possibility, however, that the *aliens* could still see lights perfectly well.

So, radio cut off and its lights extinguished, London lay under the stars of the summer night sky. At the defence posts the tense watchers stood, waiting for orders from the coordinating command before taking action. Far overhead were tiny pinpricks of light, the only visible sign of the invaders as they presumably surveyed.

Then, towards one o'clock in the morning, the first

onslaught descended. Presumably it was electromagnetic energy, in the control of which the aliens appeared to be past masters, for there swathed down on London a series of blinding spears of force, and wherever they touched stone, metal, or living flesh exploded into gas and quickly evaporated. This was the signal for the defences to open up, and they rained every known scientific bomb, shell, and beam at the drifting fireflies infinitely far overhead. They might as well have not wasted their time, for around the alien ships there immediately came into being those glowing shells of repulsive energy that harmlessly deflected everything hurled against them.

It was not clear what the aliens were trying to do. For instead of striking at London's vital points—such as the powerhouses, chemical industries, and silent radio stations—they concentrated their decimating beams upon the direct centre of the city, methodically wiping out everything in a gradually widening circle. When, by five o'clock in the morning, with the daylight commencing to appear, they had an area at least three miles in diameter swept clean in the centre of the metropolis, they called off the attack.

Only then was it clear what the idea was. From all points of the compass the alien space machines converged on this solitary, desolate area and began to descend in orderly rows. The attackers evidently meant making sure that their machines—as far as the British attack was concerned anyhow—were all in one spot. The fact that universal destruction had not occurred was hopeful, and the long-distance telephones, still untouched by the invaders, carried the news that in other countries the attackers had done precisely the same thing. Carved an area, and then descended.

On the perimeter of this great area men and women, armed as well as possible, waited for what would happen next. Those nearest the marshalled rows of spaceships watched from the windows of buildings, or from round the buildings themselves. And amongst these were Cliff and Joan. They had felt it was better to be amongst the populace than locked away in isolation. They were simply victims of the herd instinct where safety lies in numbers.

"I wonder," Joan muttered as she and Cliff gazed at the closed space machines from behind one of the huge defence barriers, "what Herbert thinks about all this?"

"Herbert!" Cliff echoed, amazed. "How, in the face of all this, can you spare the time to think of *him*?"

"Why not? He's got feelings, same as us. I'm wondering if he's still alive. Milford Park has been completely wiped out by these—these sadists!"

"We've yet to be sure that they *are* that. There's been no indiscriminate slaughter, remember. They cleared the centre of the city quite gradually. Anybody with their wits about them would have had time to run for safety. I wish they'd come out, though, and let us see what they look like. I suppose they're cooking up what to do next."

It was just as he had finished speaking that there came a sudden whirring sound from the assembled machines—or more exactly, from three of them. To the accompaniment of the sound the centre section of the three machines slid to one side, leaving the gaping rectangle of a big airlock. Beyond the openings there could dimly be seen a maze of controls and brightly glowing signal lamps. Nobody amongst the hundreds of watchers on the edge of the circle said a word: they were too fascinated. But news cameramen were still faithful enough to their jobs to quickly fit telephoto lenses and prepare to 'shoot'.

Then the first of the aliens appeared and looked about him. There was nothing horrific in his appearance. Indeed, it was difficult to tell that he was not an Earthman, except perhaps that his skin, where exposed, had a yellow-white tinge unknown in normal Earthlings unless ridden by some disease. In the case of the alien the condition was probably explained by very little ultraviolet radiation penetrating the atmosphere of his home planet. Otherwise the alien was about six feet tall, broad-shouldered, and possessed of normal arms and legs. Through camera telephoto lenses his face appeared very square, especially about the jaw, and his nose was small. His eyes were curious as they glanced around him—cat-like pupils with deep amethyst irises. Plainly he was accustomed to a world where direct, bright sunlight was unknown.

"From what I can see from here," Cliff murmured, focusing his field glasses, "he looks a pretty intelligent specimen."

Joan took the glasses from him and looked long

and earnestly, noting that the invader was dressed in a white uniform which looked rather like that of a ship's captain in tropical waters.

Then other aliens joined their colleague. They were of varying heights from five foot six to six feet, just as one might find in any Earthly community. The survey complete, the rearmost men turned back into their machine and at length brought to view an object resembling a camera on a tripod. The hidden men and women, peeping from every hole and corner, watched in fascinated interest, Joan and Cliff included. But after a moment or two they wished they had not been so much in the forefront, for as the curious object on the tripod began to glow with mysterious radiation, there also came from it an overwhelming magnetism.

Helpless, completely unable to save themselves, Joan, Cliff, and dozens of other men, women, and children found themselves dragged irresistibly towards that glowing instrument. They tried bracing their feet to stop their advance—and failed. As a needle leaps to a magnet, so they blundered and reeled to within a foot of the machine, and there they were pinned, breathless and angry, the centremost alien smiling coldly upon them.

Not until other aliens had closed in at the rear of the forty or fifty men so mysteriously 'magnetized,' was the instrument switched off. But even then it was no use making a break for it. The guardian aliens to the rear were all equipped with complicated-looking guns.

"I don't see anybody else particularly willing to

speak," Cliff commented as the alien looked at him steadily, "so maybe I'd better turn spokesman. I'm well fitted for it as an unofficial member of the Government."

As he talked, the alien continued to gaze at him with his amethyst eyes. It was not so much a stare of interest as of profound concentration, as though the man from the stars was trying to gather something from Cliff's mind.

"My name is Clifford Brooks, and I am an unofficial member of my country's government," Cliff said deliberately. "We could welcome you as visitors to our planet if we could only be assured that your intentions towards us are not hostile. So far we have no proof of that. Indeed everything points to the contrary."

The alien reflected for a moment and then turned aside to his colleagues. To one of them he issued instructions, and in response to them an instrument was wheeled into view on a stand. It was plainly electrical, and from it there snaked a variety of multicoloured wires.

In some nervousness Cliff stood looking at this instrument, and he tried to back away as two of the aliens came towards him with the coiled wires in their hands. For Cliff there was no escape, with the armed aliens to the rear, and at length he had to submit as the wires were affixed to his forehead and temples with sucker-like devices.

Then he lost his fear and gave a start of surprise instead. There was no pain occasioned by this strange treatment, and he could certainly hear a voice speaking to him.

"You are listening to me, my friend, through the medium of the language co-ordinator." It was the leader of the aliens speaking, his lips moving and, to all but Cliff, uttering words in a foreign tongue—but to Cliff himself every word sounded like very good English.

"We find this instrument very useful when the language difficulty crops up. By electrical processes too complicated to explain here, it converts air vibrations—created by a voice—into a form understandable to both parties. You may answer me in your own language if you wish. I shall quite understand."

"Very well then," Cliff said. "I repeat what I said before: we would be glad to welcome you to our planet if we could be sure that you are not hostile. Your blanketing of our radio transmissions—and your carving out central areas in the midst of our cities—can hardly be classed as acts of friendship!"

"Science knows no friendships, man of the third world. To the pure scientist, such as we represent, there is no human reaction whatever. Everything is weighed in the scale of mathematical postulations, and into that the intrusion of flesh-and-blood emotions cannot be permitted. We neither wish your friendship, nor have we hostility towards you. Our sole aim is the furtherance of our scientific prowess."

"That doesn't make sense!" Cliff retorted. "You must be perfectly aware that we are far behind you in scientific knowledge: how then can visiting *us* further your prowess?"

"Evidently," the alien reflected, "I did not make my meaning clear. We are not visiting *you*: we are visiting your world. You mean no more to us than insects mean to you. It is the properties of your planet which interest us, properties denied us on our own world."

Cliff did not comment. He waited to see what sort of an explanation was forthcoming. Around him the men and women were eagerly attentive. They could understand what *he* said, but the jabber of the alien was quite unintelligible. Joan, hanging on to Cliff's arm, tightened her hold.

"Don't tell him anything, Cliff! We're not the only folk in the world. Others can deal with this crowd if we hold out."

The amethyst eyes of the alien strayed to Joan and settled upon her. She became silent immediately, her heart thumping as the relentless gaze remained.

"Your world," the alien resumed abruptly, "is mature. Ours is not. The answer is as simple as that. For the basis of our power, we need coal and oil. On entering your solar system, we first examined the fourth world from your sun—but found that it was utterly deficient in both...."

Cliff recalled the earlier reports of light flashes seen on Mars; evidently they had been explosions as the aliens had been prospecting for—

"Coal and oil!" Cliff exclaimed, astounded. "You mean to tell me that a race as scientific as yours needs *coal*? And oil? What about atomic power? Don't you find that much more efficient?"

"We *do* use atomic power, but it is not the primitive and limited usage of your Earth scientists. The atom itself is forever unknowable—all theories about it are merely analogies or models. You have constructed a model based on the apparent duality of light—your model is based on particles and waves. Other civilizations, including our own, have completely different ideas about what atoms are. Our research has been purely along the lines of electromagnetic force, of which we have made ourselves the masters. Every power we possess is derived from this basic force of the universe. That you of this world have discovered atomic power based on particle theory we know full well. On that we congratulate you, but we believe our own particular forces are far ahead of yours. For instance, we have mastered interstellar travel: you have not."

Despite the desperate circumstances surrounding the invasion, Cliff was nonetheless interested in the scientific implications. "How," he asked, "was your interstellar journey to Earth possible? Since nothing can travel faster than light, it must surely have taken you many years—even centuries—to reach Earth."

"You overlook the fact that time stands still for any object moving at the speed of light—and also markedly contracts as one approaches that ultimate speed. With our mastery of electromagnetic forces, we can cross the gulfs between the stars in what—to us—is a relatively short time.... But, to deal with the matter on hand, our need on our home planet is for coal, and oil, and more coal and oil. We naturally utilise the natural forces on our planet such as wind and waves as well, but without coal and oil our generation of electricity and magnetic power is limited."

Cliff did not make any observation. He was absorbing the quite amazing truth that these masters of Science knew little or nothing of the nature of atomic power. He realised at that moment how much had been assumption—how he, and indeed the rest of the world, had assumed that these alien experts must know of, and use, atomic force. The fact that they did not showed clearly that scientific research must not necessarily be identical on two different planets. Plainly, the aliens had considered the control of electromagnetic forces much more important. Which, to Cliff, raised an issue. Was the atomic force of Earth sufficient to deal with the highly specialised electrical knowledge of these creatures?

"You have many coal and oil areas on this planet," the alien resumed. "Or, more correctly, fossilised trees and life-forms respectively. Our studies of this world through many years have satisfied us that you have coal and oil in abundance. We originate from a planet that is slow to reach maturity. It is still in the main in the era that you refer to as Jurassic or Carboniferous. That is, the vast coal forests which you once possessed in a bygone age—and which have formed the coal deposits of today—are with us still *forests*, and will remain so for untold generations to come. Here and there we have found coal and oil deposits, but the supply is running out. That is why we are here, to make use of your immense resources."

"Without our permission? Without so much as attempting to come to some agreement with us?" Cliff demanded. "How would *you* like it if we descended in hordes upon *your* world and decided to take whatever we wanted?"

"That does not enter into it, because your race has not the intelligence to cross interstellar space, and certainly not the intelligence to overpower us. We are accustomed to taking what we want—but I would make it clear here and now that we have no hostility to you as living beings. As I said before, neither hostility nor friendship. You simply do not enter into our calculations. We will remove what coal we detect, and thereafter leave you in peace. That is one reason why we have brought so many spaceships, so they can be loaded. The number of journeys we may have to make does not signify, but coal *we must have!*"

"So must we!" Cliff snapped. "If you think we'll stand idly by whilst you and your race do as you like, you're vastly mistaken."

The alien gave a slow, hard smile. "If you wish for a battle of scientific powers, my friend, you can assuredly have it—but you would be well advised not to try. As I understand, from radio broadcasts we picked up long ago, you are a professional mining engineer and geologist. As such you must have a very good knowledge of where coal and oil deposits are to be located."

"Quite correct—but if you are such masterminds,

why call on my feeble knowledge? Surely you have detectors which can show you where coal and oil is?"

"Most certainly we have, but there are limits to their depths of detection. You have considerable knowledge of a machine for underground exploration—a borer I believe it is called."

"Tell me," Cliff said slowly, "is it coincidence that you happened to pick on me just here, or did you *know* you would?"

"We knew," the alien answered. "Mathematical prediction of events made it inevitable. We have decided to use you as our guide."

"Then you're wasting your time!" Cliff's jaw set stubbornly.

Joan, though she could not understand the statements being made by the alien, knew perfectly well from Cliff's answers that danger was threatening him. She gave him a quick inquiring look.

"What do they want?" she demanded, and Cliff glanced at her.

"Coal and oil! All we've got—and probably a borer too, so they can find the best places! They haven't a hope."

"Since you consider yourself a person of responsibility," the alien resumed, "you must also assume everything that that responsibility implies. If you do not tell us where the best coal and oil areas are, we shall find them ourselves, but it will take much longer, and in the process we are liable to destroy great areas of this planet in order to lay bare the necessary deep deposits.

That may also involve the fissuring of volcanic seams, as you are probably aware."

"Do as you like," Cliff retorted. "I'm not helping you in the slightest degree."

For this kind of response he fully expected some excruciating scientific persuasion to be used; but to his surprise, and relief, the alien signalled for the 'interpreting' apparatus to be removed. The guards to the rear also ceased their surveillance, and returned to the space machine, disappearing within. Cliff, Joan, and the men and women grouped around them watched in silence as the alien leader made a final slow survey, then he too turned into the vessel, and the airlock, once all external apparatus had been withdrawn, closed tightly.

"This," Cliff said, taking a deep breath, "is easier than I had expected! I thought they'd try and make me tell them something, but evidently they realise it's no use—"

He broke off with a cry of warning and flung himself flat as with a sudden blasting roar the leader space machine began its skyward trek. Behind it, belching gases and poisonous fumes, swept the remainder of the assembled fleet, until in the space of perhaps ten minutes not one remained in the great area which had been blasted clean during the night.

As the last scream died away into silence on the early morning air, Cliff got slowly to his feet and helped Joan to hers. They looked about them on the men and women gradually assuming normal upright positions.

"And what happens now?" Joan asked.

"I'm not sure; but this much I do know. We have been given enough leeway to turn around, and they're certainly not going to steal our coal and oil reserves without paying dearly for everything they get. They haven't got atomic force, and we have. In a battle between electromagnetism and atomic force there's a chance we might win."

"They haven't got atomic force?" Joan repeated in wonder, and at that Cliff gave a rueful smile.

"Sorry, I keep forgetting the conversation was one-sided!" And for the sake of everybody present,1 he went into a detailed repetition of his exchange of information with the alien. When it was over, Joan was looking troubled.

"This puts you in a very nasty position," she said, thinking.

"Why *me* especially? Far as I can see, everybody is more or less threatened by whatever is going to happen next."

"I don't mean it in that sense. I mean that this alien leader has pushed all the blame on to you—and he'll take care to let everybody know that he and his race can easily accomplish their object without undue discomfort to us, *if* you will tell all you know about coal and oil areas. When the public—which is only concerned with itself anyway—learns that you're obstinate, you'll get the blame for whatever massacres may follow."

Cliff shrugged. "All right, so I get the blame. I'm not concerned with what the public thinks; only with our coal and oil reserves, and I'm mighty sure the high-ups will support me—"

Joan said no more. This was a matter that had moved beyond her province. Then one of the men amongst the assembled people came forward.

"Any suggestions as to what we ought to do next, Mr. Brooks? Or maybe you're no wiser than any of us."

"Not very much wiser certainly," Cliff admitted. "All I can suggest is that you carry on as usual. The normal life of a community has to go on, otherwise there'll be chaos. Far as I am concerned, I'm going straight to Whitehall to see whether my particular stand in this matter meets with approval or not. Then, Joan, we'd better get back home and try to live as close to normal as possible."

CHAPTER SEVEN
HERBERT THE KINGPIN

The high-ups entirely agreed with Cliff's decision. The very *thought* of bowing before an invader, because he happened to be extremely well versed in electro-magnetism, was not to be thought of. Not so much as a single speck of coal or drop of oil was to be allowed to be moved away from the Earth. If the invaders wanted to make an issue of it, the massed defences of Earth stood ready. So, immediately, the War Ministry, with intense sagacity, moved all its defence equipment and men to the main coal and offshore oil areas of Britain, and in other countries similar moves were made.

What nobody seemed to grasp—except Joan, who was always pretty quick to see through a subtlety—was that the alien leader had made a very clever move. Not having been given the information he wanted, he had compelled Earth to deliberately pinpoint the relevant areas by surrounding them with defences! Without doubt the man from space would have made a brilliant chess player.

The curious thing was that the aliens, after their initial descent and sweeping clear the centre of the major cities, seemed to vanish! Certainly there were no reports of them anywhere on Earth, and the assiduous astronomers could not spot them either. But in truth the aliens were not so very far away. They were in orbit above the Earth's surface—every ship of them, moving with the Earth's rotation so that they remained constantly on the daylight side. By his means they avoided astronomical observation, the day sky completely blinding the observers. In addition they generated an electromagnetic field that negated detection by radar.

And their reason for this hole-and-corner act? Purely and simply the age-old strategy of lulling the enemy into a sense of false security.

"Without a doubt," the alien leader commented to his followers, in the commanding vessel, "these people are by no means experts in the subtler ramifications of defence, otherwise they would not move all their material to the coal and oil areas and leave their cities denuded."

The second-in-command smiled coldly as he surveyed the cloudless Earth infinitely far below.

"It might be a good idea, Select One, to destroy those undefended cities one by one as a measure of the power we possess."

"Don't talk like a fool! To destroy even one city would tax our electromagnetic energy considerably: to destroy the lot would leave us without resources with which to obtain that which we need most—coal and oil. You have too great a liking of destruction for destruction's sake, my friend."

"My apologies, Select One. It was only a thought."

"What we *might* do," the leader said, thinking, "is to have the dampening effect on this planet's radio removed. That will serve the double purpose of making these fools think we have departed and restored their normal facilities; and it will also make us able to hear what plans they have for combating us. Those who do not think they are overheard speak freely."

The second-in-command nodded promptly; and gave the order to the nearby radio operator; then he looked back at his thoughtful superior.

"I trust, Select One, that you are not delaying too long? The more we hold our attack in abeyance the more time these people have to strengthen their defences."

"Such as they are," the leader answered dryly. "They feel secure in the knowledge that they have atomic power—yet how much use is it? They endeavoured to strike at us with it upon our arrival—but what happened? Our electromagnetic repulsion screens made us invulnerable. No, I am not delaying too long. I am waiting for that supreme moment when they no longer believe we mean to attack, even for the moment when they decide to remove their defences from the coal and oil areas. We have those areas clearly marked, so we know exactly where to strike."

"Do you really believe," the second-in-command asked, "that the people will turn on this being Clifford Brooks and force him to tell us what we want to know? It would be a great help if he would, for he must know of areas which surface defences do not mark out."

"We must be patient and see how matters work out. Once we start into action I am sure that, rather than have their planet ploughed up and desecrated, these people will compel the man Clifford Brooks to talk. Frankly," the Select One continued, sighing, "I am not particularly in favour with any part of this appropriation, even as I told the Ultimate before we departed. No good can come of invading another's territory. History has shown us that, and I have not forgotten that only a few hours before our departure there was much restiveness from the forest gods. Always a bad sign, my friend; always a bad sign."

"True," the second-in-command admitted gloomily. "The forest gods are so right, and we do not heed them often enough. Animals they may be, and female at that, but they have instincts denied to us."

The Select One nodded sombrely and did not speak. His mind was back in the steaming Carboniferous forests of his own planet, wherein wandered the beasts whom the alien 'humans' regarded as sacred because of their immensely long lives. Which revealed but another facet of these extraordinary alien people. On the one hand they had supreme scientific advancement, yet on the other an intense pagan devotion to the monsters who lived in the as yet uncleared areas of their world.... Truly, progress had developed in a strange way on their alien planet, at least by comparison with Earth standards. Yet who can say that the Earth standard is the *correct* one?

And, down on the surface of the Earth, as no further attack seemed to be coming—and as radio magically returned to life—there came a gradual lessening of tension, and in the defence areas a slow relaxation of vigilance, chiefly because of sheer boredom. The Select One's idea of creating a sense of false security was working out very nicely.

"If you ask me," Cliff told Joan, as week succeeded week and nothing happened, "it was my speech that scared them off! They realised from what I told them that we're well away with atomic force, and I'll warrant that caused them to pack up their traps and clear off."

Joan shook her head absently. "Masters of electro-magnetism don't need to pack up, Cliff. Stop fooling yourself! They'll come back, and when they do I'll gamble they'll blow this old planet of ours wide apart!"

But Cliff was not convinced. Manlike, he was on the crest of a wave of optimism, and convinced that his own forthright speaking had averted disaster. He had not Joan's gift for sensing what lay below the surface.

"In any case," Joan resumed presently, as the evening meal proceeded in the late summer twilight, "I'm not too concerned about the aliens at the moment. I'm thinking of Herby."

"What about him?"

"That's just it! I don't know *anything* about him! When the aliens swept the centre of London clean, they destroyed Milford Park in the process and Herbert hasn't been seen since. I can think of only one answer to that: he was killed outright. I mean, it isn't as though he's some small creature who could easily escape detection. If he broke loose from Milford Park and escaped death, he'd surely have been seen by now?"

"Yes, I suppose so," Cliff admitted soberly. "Pity in some ways. He wasn't such a bad beast, wasn't old Herby. On the other hand, maybe it's a blessing for him and for us. He was pretty lonely without a mate, and we didn't know what to do with him."

Joan sighed and went on with her meal. Her position was such that she looked beyond Cliff, at the opposite side of the table, towards the french windows. They were open, as indeed they had been throughout this long, blazing summer. Outside, the twilight sky was beginning to show a sprinkling of stars—until something enormous suddenly blotted out the view.

Joan gave a start and blinked. Cliff looked at her in surprise as she sat rigid, her knife and fork in mid-air.

"What the blazes is the matter *now?*" Cliff demanded impatiently.

"It's—it's *Herbert*!" Joan managed to gasp out; and at that she sprang up, overturning her chair in her excitement, and dashed to the open windows. Cliff twisted his head to follow her movements.

"Yes, it *is* he!" Joan cried back at him, and she ran quickly through the french windows towards a mighty pillar of grey which was obscuring the stars. Immediately Cliff got up and went to investigate.

There was now no longer any doubt about the matter. Outside in the starlight stood Herbert, his huge tongue sweeping down to give his eager mistress an unwanted wash. She turned quickly to Cliff in the reflected light, the front of her summery dress splashed and stained with the activities of Herbert's ferocious kissing.

"Now I wonder where the devil he's been," Cliff mused, gazing up at the stupendous head at roof level. "Like you said, Joan, he's not exactly insignificant."

Joan did not answer. The first enthusiasm of the greeting over she ran around the huge beast, gazing at him intently. Finally she pointed to dark streaks of mud that had settled in the armour-clad skin.

"He's been underground, I think," she said. "There hasn't been any rain for some weeks, so he'd hardly collect any mud. You're the geologist of the family: what's your diagnosis?"

Cliff went into the house for a torch, then at the end of his inspection he nodded quickly.

"Good guess on your part, Joan. This sort of mud is only found about a mile below surface. Unless I miss my guess Herby must have got clear of Milford Park before or during the onslaught on central London. Probably panicked and sheer strength enabled him to smash the railed enclosure down—"

"But one of those fences was electrified!"

"You don't suppose a thing like that would stop Herby, do you? I've seen him with a hundred thousand-volt wires wrapped around him, and the current only made him jump around happily. Not much use conjecturing anything, really, I suppose. He got free, obviously, and then maybe went down one of the craters gouged by that alien attack. That way he'd easily reach the underworld and comparative safety. I'll wager he's only come back because things are quiet again. As to how he found us, I don't know. He seems to have a peculiar instinct that way."

"It *must* be that he can smell us," Joan insisted. "Sounds awfully indelicate, I know, but—animals are peculiar that way."

"And now, I suppose he wants something to eat," Cliff sighed. "Better ring up the abattoirs, Joan, and—"

Cliff broke off suddenly, staring into the starry sky that lay over London. Joan looked with him and immediately she saw that which had claimed his attention. Over the city—at present at a considerable altitude, but rapidly dropping lower—were what looked like glowing balls ejected from a monstrous Roman candle. There were perhaps fifty—no, a hundred of them, descending swiftly.

"Over there, too!" Joan exclaimed, swinging round and pointing.

For that matter the whole sky had suddenly become alive with the drifting shapes. The greatest concentration was obviously over the city, but the environs had not by any means escaped. Almost at the same moment there came the distant sound of exploding atomic ack-ack shells.

"It looks as though your guess was right, sweetheart." Cliff gripped Joan tightly about the shoulders as they stared aloft together. "Those blasted aliens have returned."

Herbert, apparently sensing danger, swung his head

back and forth, sniffing the breeze. Then he let loose an overpowering roar which made the ground shake.

"Quiet, Herby!" Joan insisted, suddenly nervy. "Things are strained enough without that row!"

Herbert took no notice. He kneaded his huge front feet and bellowed again; then apparently seized with an overpowering instinct of danger, he swung about and went galloping across the lawn. It was not possible to follow his movements for long in the uncertain light, but there did presently come the sound of railings collapsing as he ploughed through them.

"Scare baby!" Joan called after him scornfully. "You'd think a creature as big as him would—"

"Animal instinct is keener than ours, Joan," Cliff interrupted her. "He's got some good *reason* for behaving like that. I wonder if *that* could be it?" he broke off, pointing aloft.

Joan gazed overhead. One of the bright globes had detached itself from the others and was streaking with incredible velocity straight towards where the two stood. Or at least it seemed that way. Much of the effect was the illusion presented by the bubble of colour around the object, but there was no doubting the fact that it presently dropped to Earth, not far from Herbert's hangar in the field beyond. When that happened, the glowing colour globe expired.

"It's the aliens, all right," Cliff said grimly. "The colour globes will be the shell of repulsive energy with which they sheath themselves— And from the look of things," he added, with a quick glance around the sky, "the rest of 'em have landed, too. Better get back in the house. I don't like the idea of that particularly near one."

Neither of them hesitated any longer. They had almost forgotten all about Herbert, so intent were they on their own safety. But Herbert had not forgotten them. Nor had he deserted them. It had simply been that overwhelming instinct had urged him to move quickly from what he sensed was to become a danger spot. That urge had gone now, and he stood sniffing the breeze, his baleful red eyes fixed on the vision of a space machine not very far from his locked hangar-home. That, he felt, was where the danger lay—and in this he was right, for the aliens possessed, even in small arms, enough electromagnetic energy to blow the king of dinosaurs from the face of the Earth.

No, Herbert wasn't having any. Still with nostrils twitching he dropped down on his forelegs, elephant-wise, and then rolled on his side. In this position he was not visible in the starlight, except to look like a rising mound. Thus he lay, his ultra-fine sense of smell catching the drift from the distant space machine as an airlock opened and a tiny pencil of light jetted into the night.

The Select One and his colleagues, weapons strapped to their waists, stood looking about them. For them, everything was going perfectly. They had at last launched their drive for coal and oil, taking the precaution at the same time to paralyse the main centre from which danger might come—namely London. So it was in all those countries where coal and oil was known to exist in large quantities. The nearest cities had been attacked whilst other machines travelled to the nearest coal centres. In London, indeed, the battle was joined in earnest, the noise of it drifting on the night air like a thunderstorm. Perpetual flashes of light over and in the metropolis gave the clue as to what kind of man-made tempest was raging there.

"There is no point in ignoring the possibilities of this man Clifford Brooks," the Select One said, as his colleagues joined him. "He has specialised knowledge of coal locations far below the surface and therefore out of reach of our detectors. It is time he gave us the information we required. Apparently it is of no use waiting for the people to turn on him, as we had at first hoped— If he should prove stubborn, we can doubtless force him to speak by means of his wife. Come!"

There was no longer any hesitation on the part of the men from space. Leaving two of their number in charge of the space machine, they stepped out across the darkened meadow, moving steadily in the direction of the Brooks' home. Herbert raised his huge head to watch them go, then his eyes turned in the direction of the space machine. Clumsily, he presently got to his feet. Here was something that needed investigation.

The two aliens left in charge of the space machine had no intimation as to the coming of Herbert, for, not anticipating interference, their detector instruments had been switched off. Therefore, the first warning they received that all was not as it should be came when the vessel began to rock slightly.

Sharply the two aliens looked at one another.

"Explosion blast?" one of them suggested sharply, but the other shook his head. The city was too far away for the blast to have travelled this far, and at the moment there were no explosions nearer than those in the metropolis.

"Look!" the second one whispered in amazement, and he pointed to the open airlock. His colleague gazed, and then started.

Outside there was a solitary grey-skinned leg, as massive as a pillar. It moved as the two men looked, and the space machine jolted again.

"This is impossible!" the first alien declared blankly. "Monster beasts no longer exist on this planet—"

Leaving his sentence unfinished and tugging one of his lethal weapons from his belt, he hurried to the airlock and peered outwards and upwards. At the same instant a bellowing roar shook the night and a titanic head came sweeping down. Around the airlock, murderous, triple-toothed jaws snapped shut.

Startled, the alien fell back into the control room, firing his gun savagely. He took no particular aim in his panic, but the searing pencil did glance across Herbert's sensitive nose and stung him viciously. Instantly he kicked out with his mighty feet, rocking the space ship violently and sending both aliens reeling against the wall.

"A monster—here!" the first one gasped, struggling up. "I do not understand it, unless he is gifted with godlike powers like those of our own world—"

"Godlike or otherwise, he's dangerous!" the second alien cut in. "Get the ship away before he wrecks it!"

"But—but what of the Select One?"

"We'll return for him afterwards. Give this beast time to get away from this region."

The first alien hesitated no longer as the furious Herbert kicked, butted, and charged the space machine. He was hurt and frightened and angry, and he knew that if he pondered long enough he could smash this space vessel like an old tin. But he was not given the opportunity. The airlock abruptly closed and then amidst a flaring of jet exhausts the machine took to the air, covering Herbert transiently in a deluge of sparks. He yelped again and then reared his mighty head upwards. Already the space ship was cleaving to the upper heights, its passage marked by a thin line of crumbling fire.

The Select One and his colleagues, who at this moment had reached the grounds of the Brooks' home, came to a stop and stared aloft in amazement; then they glanced at each other in the starlight.

"Strange," the Select One commented, puzzled. "Inza and Gioj were instructed to wait for us. Why, I wonder, have they taken off?"

"Possibly some kind of danger threatening," his first-in-command responded. "If they do not return we have nothing to fear, not with so many of our machines on this planet."

"If they *do* return," the Select One observed bitterly,

"it is to be hoped for their own sakes that they have a reasonable explanation for such strange behaviour.... But come, we waste time."

They went forward again, and in another moment had entered the dining room through the open french windows. Since it was the only ground floor room with lights showing, it had naturally led the aliens to make for it. Now they stood with their weapons levelled, gazing at Cliff and Joan as they sat making an end of their evening meal.

"Evidently I was right," Cliff muttered, watching narrowly. "I said I didn't like the prospect of that very near spaceship."

As he finished speaking, the Select One made a quick motion to his first-in-command, which resulted in there being brought into view a small-sized edition of a language-interpreter. Cliff sat motionless as the Select One, covered by his colleagues' weapons, came forward with the instrument in his hands. In a matter of moments connections had been made to Cliff's head.

He made no protest, knowing from previous experience that the operation was quite painless. Joan looked on tensely, powerless to do anything to help the situation.

"Does my language make sense to you?" the Select One asked, after a moment.

"Entirely," Cliff acknowledged. "I've a pretty good idea why you've sought me out again, too! It's to get some information about those coal seams and oil deposits, isn't it?"

"I am glad you have so quickly grasped the situation."

The Select One came closer, his colleagues grouped around him. All of them were unsmiling, their weapons steadily levelled.

"Allow me to compliment you on your strategy!" Cliff said bitterly. "You kept away long enough to make everybody think you'd departed for home—then you return when we're not expecting and destroy everything in sight! But we'll beat you to it yet—and don't you forget it!"

"We shall take what we came for," the Select One stated. "Be assured of that—but from you we require specialised information. The surface areas of coal that we have located—and that have been revealed to us by the depth of the defences out around them—are by no means sufficient for our purpose. What *other* areas are there and how do we get at them?"

"You can only get at them with a borer, and there are none of those available. As to where the areas are—I'm keeping that to myself and you can do your worst!"

The Select One gave his mirthless smile. "I can assure you our worst can be very painful indeed. Does it not mean anything to you that you can stop the attack on your cities simply by telling us what we wish to know?"

"How would *that* stop the attack?" Cliff demanded, puzzled.

"It would stop because we would have no machines or men to maintain the onslaught. Every machine and every man would be required to deal with the coal and oil areas. Our attack would change to defence as we safeguarded ourselves against those trying to prevent us removing the coal and oil we so desperately need."

Cliff laughed shortly. "Excuse me if I say I don't believe a word of it! And I'm *not* telling you anything, so don't waste your time."

"I do not altogether believe, my friend, that the issue is entirely up to you! There is your wife to think of— to say nothing of the hundreds of thousands who can be spared if you will tell us what we wish to know. It would be unfortunate if, for instance, in our search for the deeper areas of coal, we left not a single living being on this planet. And that, I assure you, is more than a possibility."

Cliff shook his head stubbornly. "If you wish to destroy everybody on this planet, you'll try and do it anyway, whether I speak or not."

"Very well." The Select One gave a shrug and then looked at Joan. Since she had only heard Cliff's side of the conversation she was not aware of how things stood—but she guessed pretty quickly when, at a signal, the alien immediately behind her put his forearm under her chin and thus pinned her head immovably.

Instantly Cliff sprang to his feet, dislodging the voice-interpretative apparatus in the process. However, before he could move to help the vainly struggling Joan he was flung back into his chair by the nearest alien and the apparatus returned to his skull.

"You should know better," the Select One

commented. Then after a pause he added: "You can save your wife a great deal of discomfort, not to say pain, if you do as you have been asked."

Joan squirmed savagely, but she could not break free. Her terrified face turned to Cliff over the relentless arm of the alien.

"I suppose it's coal and oil they're after?" she panted.

"Right," Cliff told her. "And if I don't tell them all they want to know, heaven knows what they'll do to you—so I've got to speak."

"No, Cliff! Don't let them scare you into it. I can take it, whatever's coming—"

Cliff hesitated, then he watched in horrified fascination as the Select One withdrew a glittering instrument from the belt of equipment around his waist. The object looked rather like a hypodermic syringe, only it was much more complicated. Presumably it was electrical, like all the other instruments used by these ruthless people.

"I have here an instrument which can gradually destroy the operation of any nervous system," the Select One explained. "The needle end is driven into the main nerve root and after that electricity does the rest. The process is excruciating, and the consequences quite tragic. In a matter of five minutes the sight and hearing are destroyed, and after that the whole nervous system's control breaks down, resulting in a blind, deaf, incurable paralytic—I trust I make myself clear?"

"You're not going to use that damned thing on my wife!" Cliff yelled, and with a sudden tremendous surge he dragged to his feet and slammed round his fist. It hit the nearest alien straight on the nose and sent him staggering backwards....

But this was as far as Cliff could get. Though he thrashed out blindly with his fists and landed a fair amount of punishment in the process, he was finally forced back into his chair and there held, not by one alien but three.

"All right, you win," he muttered, panting. "We can't fight your kind of technique. I'll tell you all you want to know."

"Good!" the Select One murmured, returning the instrument to his belt. "Release the woman!"

This was done, paper and pen were brought from the bureau, and then Cliff sat hunched and thoughtful with Joan looking at him anxiously.

"Why *do* you give in to them?" she asked hopelessly. "It's only staving off the—"

"I can't let them kill you by inches, can I?" Cliff snapped. "You don't know what was intended: *I* do! I know what I'm doing."

With that he began to sketch rapidly, drawing a design of the world with the various countries clearly marked. The Select One and his colleagues watched interestedly, only glancing up occasionally as a particularly heavy reverberation came from the direction of London.

Fifteen minutes passed...twenty. Then at the end of an hour Cliff had done. He handed the drawing up to the Select One.

"And this," the alien asked, "comprises the main coal and oil-bearing areas of your planet?"

"Yes—above and below ground. As I told you earlier, we have no borers which can go to the underworld regions and investigate those strata I've marked there; but I don't doubt your science will be up to finding a way."

"Doubtless," the alien agreed, "and I would remark, my friend, that this sketch had better be *correct*. If it is not, I shall return and no matter where you may go you will not escape me."

"It's genuine enough," Cliff sighed. "You don't suppose I'd take a gamble with the life of my wife, do you?"

The alien said no more. He seemed satisfied. The language interpreter was removed from Cliff's head, and without commenting further, the aliens stepped out into the night. Cliff watched them go, tiny lines of worry round his eyes. After an interval Joan came over to him.

"You realise what you've done?" she asked quietly.

"I realise I've saved you from a living death—and nothing else matters."

"I appreciate that you've done the best as far as *I* am concerned, but I'm only one person amongst millions. How do you suppose civilisation is going to fare when every scrap of coal and oil has been removed?"

Cliff gave a shrug. "If I hadn't done as they asked, it would have meant the end of civilisation anyway, and most certainly the end of you. I've taken the line of least resistance, Joan."

She said nothing, anxious on the one hand for the ultimate fate of the human race, yet grateful on the other that Cliff placed her above everybody else in importance. And meanwhile, the aliens were returning across the starlit meadow to their space machine, or at least to the location where they had left it. When they beheld it in the distance, its portholes lighted, they wondered if the machine they had seen climbing into the night sky had been *this* one after all.

And, a quarter of a mile away, the world's largest dinosaur was sniffing the breeze and trying to sum things up in his own ponderous way.

Smiling to himself, the Select One entered the control room and then turned in surprise as one of the two men he had left in charge came hurrying towards him.

"Select One, an incredible thing has happened!"

"Indeed? Surely not incredible enough to warrant such an unseemly display of emotion! Remember, we are trained to—"

"There exists upon this world a monster! A dinosaur! And from what I have seen, this monster is *male!*"

The Select One's expression slowly changed. Behind him his colleagues waited expectantly.

"This monster is similar in appearance and size to the female monsters of our own forests," the alien continued. "How he comes to exist on a world like this I do not know, since such animals should have vanished millions of years ago. But he *does* exist, Select One! He came near to wrecking this very machine, so we took to the air in order to escape him. When we returned, there was no sign of him."

The Select One reflected. That this machine *had* taken to the sky was now verified. But this monster...?

"You did not see any of his footprints, Select One?" the second guardian alien asked quickly.

"No, but we soon can. Switch on the searchlight!" Instantly a blaze of light flooded the area around the space machine, and in the effulgence the deeply sunken tracks of Herbert's immense feet were clearly visible. The Select One's face became thoughtful.

"This grows interesting," he said at last. "The female beasts of our own world are doomed to extinction, now that the male has died out. Here, perhaps, is a chance of perpetuation. The beasts are sacred, and as they die, so must our fortunes decline. If we can but keep their species living, our progress will continue."

"True, Select One," the first-in-command agreed quickly.

Upon which the Select One came to a decision. He stepped out of the airlock and then glanced back.

"I will see this Earthman again, and see if he can explain the presence of a monster on this planet. Wait for me."

With that he strode away actively under the stars, a lethal weapon in his hand. It was too dark now for him to see the mighty beast which had picked up his scent, too dark for him to see that Herbert was following slowly, his suspicions at last aroused sufficiently for him to get on the move.

Cliff and Joan were talking earnestly together and listening to the concussions of war from distant London when the Select One strode in upon them for the second time that evening. In a matter of moments he had fixed the portable language-interpreter on Cliff's head.

"Now what?" Cliff asked sourly. "There's nothing more I can tell you regarding coal and oil deposits."

"They are not my interest this time, Earthman. You have on this planet a beast of a past era. My colleagues have seen it, but I have not."

Cliff looked surprised. "Yes, certainly we have. He happens to be a particular pet of my wife and myself. Why, how does that concern you?"

"You said—*he*?"

"I did. He's one hundred percent male."

"That being so, he will be appropriated. We of our world have many similar beasts, all female, and they hold a sacred position in our society. We believe our fortune—or the reverse—is governed by them. We do not wish them to die out, nor need they since this happy accident of discovering a male beast of similar genus on this world. Where do I find this creature?"

Cliff frowned. "I would have thought that creatures of different *worlds* could not mate successfully. Even here on Earth, different *species* are unable to—"

"That is irrelevant, " the Select One snapped. "With our mastery of genetic engineering at the molecular level, we can very soon make them compatible. I repeat my question: where can I find the creature?"

Cliff did not answer. He was thinking that some-where here there ought to be a bargaining weapon. On the one hand there was lonely Herbert, apparently longing for some of his own kind, particularly female. Then there was the matter of wanting to be rid of him because of the expense and upkeep.... On the other hand, there was an alien demanding all the coal and oil on Earth and Herbert as well.

"May I consult my wife?" Cliff questioned finally. "She is as much involved as I am concerning the dino-saur."

"Yes, consult her," the alien assented—so Cliff turned and gave Joan the details.

"You don't have Herbert at any price!" she declared flatly, but since she was not wearing the language-interpreter, her statement had no effect.

"My wife is not agreeable," Cliff said. "The monster is our pet—"

"This is absurd!" the Select One snapped. "You cannot keep a valuable sacred creature as a pet when on another world the female of his species demands his presence! Where is he to be found, or must I again use persuasion to extract the information?"

Cliff did not answer, so without waiting any longer, the alien strode to the unsuspecting Joan and seized her arm tightly. So tremendous was the pressure exerted she could not tear herself free. She was held closely to the alien as he pressed his lethal weapon into her side.

"The choice is yours, Earthman," he said. "Tell me where this monster is to be found, or else your wife will—"

The screaming roar that came from outside drowned out the rest of the alien's statement. He twirled in alarm, his weapon ready, flinging Joan away from him. Simultaneously a mighty grey head crashed down through the french windows—and through the wall above them. The alien fell on his back, aiming his gun and firing livid energy at that huge tunnel armed with triple teeth.

Herbert jolted, screeched with pain as the weapon's searing pencil bit into the roof of his mouth. But he did not change position. His mighty legs straddled the Select One as he still lay on the floor, trying to aim his weapon.

"Herbert!" Joan shouted frantically. "Herbert! Stop! Behave yourself!"

The head lifted slightly and the blazing red eyes, homicidal at the thought of the danger that had been hovering over his mistress, masked a little. There were always liquid depths in those ferocious orbs when they looked upon the tiny Earth woman who had always been kind to him.

Cliff quickly adjusted the language-interpreter on his head and knelt beside the prostrated and plainly terrified alien. He had given up trying to aim his gun, realising it was useless against an ironclad like this.

"Here he is," Cliff said. "You wanted the dinosaur— here he is! How do you propose to 'appropriate' him? Believe me, he won't go anywhere unless my wife tells him. She is the only person on this planet who can control him!"

"Force can drive him!" the alien panted. Then he seemed to think swiftly. "No, I am forgetting. One does not use force upon a sacred animal. Either he goes as the gods direct, or he doesn't go at all."

Cliff reflected, trying to assimilate the extraordinary fact that the scientific aliens worshipped prehistoric monsters. Yet, why not? He recalled instances of highly intelligent Earth men, and women too, worshipping all kinds of weird objects.... Simply a matter of theological tendency....

"Give me that language thing!" Joan said abruptly, so Cliff obliged. Once the exchange was made, Joan knelt on the floor beside the alien and eyed him steadily. Then she glanced up at the towering beast forming a bridge above them, his head just clear of the lofty dining room ceiling.

"Up, Herby!" she commanded, and instantly one front leg rose. Thereafter, under Joan's directions, the underside of the front foot, armed with its terrible claws, manoeuvred around until it was poised like a suspended trip-hammer two feet above the alien's terrified face.

"Now, my friend," Joan said deliberately, "One word from me will bring Herbert's foot down upon you, and that will smash your head to a pulp! So apparently the bargaining side is now *mine*! You say you want this great beast. I am prepared to let you take him because I think he needs his own kind, and also because I know, since he is regarded as sacred, that he will be well treated and revered. I am prepared to direct him to your space ship—and he will obey me implicitly—but after that he will be your own responsibility. I can also hypnotically impress upon him the command that he must destroy you if you do not keep the promise you are about to give to me." The hypnosis business was sheer bluff, but Joan was gambling that the alien could not be sure that it was.

"What promise?" the alien asked quickly, his eyes fixed on that still poised foot as Herbert loomed awkwardly on three legs.

"The promise to leave this world of ours immediately, with all your men and machines, leaving your coal and oil mission unfulfilled! If you do that, you shall have your sacred dinosaur and let him perpetuate your sacred animal race. If you do not, your animal race will slowly die because there are no males, and you too will die because I shall tell Herbert to drop his foot. Now choose! The animal is getting tired!"

The alien hesitated, perspiring freely. The mighty foot lowered a little as Herbert growled complainingly.

"I agree!" The Select One gasped the words out quickly. "Have this monster move away so I may radio my colleagues."

"To one side, Herbert," Joan ordered, and he backed away clumsily, pushing his rear quarters clean through the fireplace. There he stood, waiting, his red eyes fixed on the alien as he fiddled nervously with his pocket radio apparatus. What he said was not intelligible, since Joan had removed the language-interpreter, but within minutes there was visible confirmation in the endless streaks that flashed to the heavens as the vast alien fleet, its mission incomplete, took to the void and left Earth behind.

It was nearing two in the morning before the last spaceship had gone, and over the radio there came the information that for reasons unknown the invaders had departed. The Select One gave a grim smile and motioned Joan to return the language-interpreter to her head.

"I have kept my word," he said. "Now I expect you to keep yours."

"I intend to," she answered coldly. "Will your space machine hold a monster this size?"

"There will be room for him in the belly of the ship where we had intended to put coal or oil."

"Very well." Joan glanced up at the half-asleep beast and prodded his foreleg with her shoe. "Move, Herby! Follow mama."

Herbert snuffled and began moving. In a moment the strange procession—an Earth man and woman, a dinosaur, and an alien—was marching across the dark field beyond the estate, and they kept on going until the spaceship was reached. Here, under the Select One's directions, the side of the vessel was opened and beyond it lay quarters large enough for Herbert to move—within limits—until he reached the steaming jungle wastes of an alien planet.

"Remember," Joan said deliberately, fixing on the headset once more. "This beast will turn on you if you ever come back with thoughts of stealing our——"

"We shall not come back," the alien interrupted. "To do so would go against the wish of the sacred ones. We will find some other source of power, though it will not be easy. Weighed in the balance, a sacred male is more important than power for us. If we have the sacred beasts, we shall also have progress."

With that he took the headset and stowed it in his belt. Cliff and Joan looked at the huge beast in the gloom. He sounded to be whimpering.

"Nothing to worry about, old man," Joan told him, giving his huge leg a gentle stroke. "You're going among the ladies and you'll have the time of your life! Bye, Herby, and God bless you!"

The side of the machine closed. Joan backed away, Cliff's arm about her shoulder, then with a sudden blinding flare of exhaust and poisonous fumes the space machine began its diagonal sweep towards the heavens.

Silent, Cliff and Joan watched that 'S' of sparks cleave to the zenith; then it was gone.

"Let's go," Cliff murmured at last. "Good old Herby doesn't know it, but he probably saved the world!"

"Which bears out what the Reverend Maxwell said," Joan answered slowly. "He said Herby was 'Providential.' Sent for a *purpose*! Now we know what that purpose was...!"

ABOUT THE AUTHOR

British writer JOHN RUSSELL FEARN was born near Manchester, England, in 1908. As a child he devoured the science fiction of Wells and Verne, and was a voracious reader of the Boys' Story Papers. He was also fascinated by the cinema, and first broke into print in 1931 with a series of articles in *Film Weekly*.

He then quickly sold his first novel, *The Intelligence Gigantic*, to the American magazine, *Amazing Stories*. Over the next fifteen years, writing under several pseudonyms, Fearn became one of the most prolific contributors to all of the leading US science fiction pulps, including such legendary publications as *Astounding Stories*, *Startling Stories*, *Thrilling Wonder Stories*, and *Weird Tales*.

During the late 1940s he diversified into writing novels for the UK market, and also created his famous superwoman character, The Golden Amazon, for the prestigious Canadian magazine, the Toronto *Star Weekly*. In the early 1950s in the UK, his fifty-two novels as "Vargo Statten" were bestsellers, most notably his novelization of the film, *Creature from the Black Lagoon*.

Apart from science fiction, he had equal success with westerns, romances, and detective fiction, writing an amazing total of 180 novels—most of them in a period of just ten years—before his early death in 1960. His work has been translated into nine languages, and continues to be reprinted and read worldwide.